MADMAN'S WILL

Just after the funeral of a murdered man, the murderer is shocked to find that he has been left a legacy by his victim — a bank deposit box containing some old socks, a key for a set of cut-throat razors and a number of pornographic photographs of the deceased's secretary. But why was the valueless legacy left? Did the dead man know who his murderer would be, and would the articles in the box somehow give him away?

JOHN NEWTON CHANCE

◆

MADMAN'S WILL

Complete and Unabridged

LINFORD
Leicester

First published in Great Britain in 1982 by
Robert Hale Limited
London

First Linford Edition
published 1999
by arrangement with
Robert Hale Limited
London

British Library CIP Data

Chance, John Newton, *1911 – 1983*
    Madman's will.—Large print ed.—
Linford mystery library
1. Detective and mystery stories
2. Large type books
I. Title
823.9'14 [F]

ISBN 0-7089-5605-X

Published by
F. A. Thorpe (Publishing) Ltd.
Anstey, Leicestershire

Set by Words & Graphics Ltd.
Anstey, Leicestershire
Printed and bound in Great Britain by
T. J. International Ltd., Padstow, Cornwall

This book is printed on acid-free paper

1

'Forasmuch as it hath pleased Almighty God in his great mercy to take unto himself the soul of our dear brother here departed — '

'But He didn't,' thought Rayner, staring down at the pit at his feet. '*I* did. I despatched the fatuous old clown. The Almighty decided nothing; I decided. I, standing here amongst this pathetic pretence of mourners, bashed his head in, and for certain, God had nothing at all to do with it. He didn't stop me, and He didn't inspire me. I did it, and I stand here now the master of a situation I created.'

Furtively, because he was supposed to be praying for the guidance of the worthless soul in the box, he watched the mourners with a kind of bitter pleasure at their foolishness.

Mrs Garner, the widow who had left her dear departed husband years ago,

1

now stood in the blackest weeds; thin, nondescript, staring down into the hole as if from a kind of distorted duty.

Mann, the new manager, hat in hand, grey coat, brown gloves, head bent obediently, was trying to suck a lozenge without his jaws moving. He had been stepped up to take over the dead Garner's chair. He wanted the money but not the position. He had a mistress back in Ipswich and it had been convenient as undermanager in that branch. Back here he had to live with his wife again, and he didn't like her.

'What a mess,' Rayner thought, with satisfaction.

On the opposite side of the grave stood Partridge, red-faced, staring into the distance as if trying to stop himself thinking irreverent thoughts. He was a buyer for the branch and popular with the sellers for his jokes, cheerfulness, cunning and refreshing ability to ask for, and take, hand-outs openly as if they formed part of every legitimate business deal.

The vicar intoned in competition with

the fresh April wind which was rattling littered paper across the churchyard, chasing round the tombstones, like happy, restless souls long gone, for whom a funeral made a break and some fresh flowers for a change.

And last, Rayner looked at Miss Hayworth; Hagworth he said in his head, pronouncing it viciously. Hagworth. He hated Hagworth, with a satisfying violence. He watched her tall figure, in a faultless black suit; she was elegant in figure and in stance with a bosom, as Partridge said, 'you could stand your cup of tea on'. Her hat was small, as elegant as the rest, and with a shallow black veil that reached to her nose and left the big, loose, ugly mouth for all to see.

Partridge would keep ribbing him about Hagworth. 'You're looking down, lad, what you need is a couple of hours on the Hagworth; that'll straighten you out, my boy. You know what they say, the ugly ones make up for it in the dark. In the afternoons you can put a pillow over her face.'

Suddenly he realised that, behind the

veil, Hagworth was staring at him.

An uneasiness over the unknown, which he had felt ever since the murder, began to edge into fear of the known when he realised she was watching him. Perhaps she knew.

He stared down the hole again. Hagworth had been old Garner's mistress. Everybody knew that. Everybody knew about Hagworth except her age, and guessed it as between thirty and forty; the girls said forty, the men less.

He wondered why he was not thinking of Garner and that night in the office when he had killed him. It was odd, really, that now the man was boxed up and sunk down the hole the murder was shrinking in his mind like a ghost in a film, fading back through a wall till only the panelling was left to look at.

Rayner had had enough church in his short life. He had been sent to a great school, a historic school, and his headmaster had become the Archbishop of York as a reward for marching his downtrodden pupils into church so often.

Oh, the sonorous blah, the bawling

through the high nose, the swing and hang of the intonations, incantations; Sin, sin, jolly old sin, once you've broken all ten you can rest in the bin. Sin, sin, jolly old sin; you had your share, Garner. You didn't miss anything out. It was time you went down there in a box. I decided it was time just before the Almighty did. Perhaps that makes me His right hand man now. That's why I'm not frightened. That's why I don't give one solitary, lonely, misbegotten damn. Justice has been done. Justice, justice, Garner . . . Have a care, Rayner, you are beginning to excuse everything all over again. It was a crime, a murder, and it was not retribution, however you try to twist it. You committed murder —

He saw her staring at him and his heart froze for an instant, then reheated to boiling point with fury against her. She challenged him. She was always challenging him. She challenged him even across the open grave of the man she had bedded and he had murdered. He could not see the steel-grey eyes behind the veil but he could feel she was staring at him, trying to see some tiny trace of guilt as he stood there, bareheaded at his victim's grave.

Ashes to ashes, dust to dust; back to the earth, Garner, back into the worms and decay and pollution; seep into the ground and rise up refreshed into the seeds of some beautiful flower that can be cut and pinned between the Hagworth's arrogant tits, back where you spent so many hours, Garner, in the bosom of your loveless whore.

The vicar was closing the book; he went to Mrs Garner, his white gown blowing in the wind like some dove flying to its love along the graveside.

She must have come for the will to be read. It seemed that Garner had been a stickler for convention, besides fiddling the tills, and had wished his will to be read to the invited guests. Hagworth, of course, was in command of the arrangements, Hagworth would hand round the sherry on a tray smiling firmly, with just a trace of sadness on her big, loose lips, and the thrust of command and confidence in her thrusting bosom, and the perfect placing of her beautiful long legs as she moved among the fumblers. They fumbled because nobody ever knew what to do at funerals until they got tight.

He began to move away slowly from the grave. Everyone was turning, with quiet relief, towards the cars.

★ ★ ★

Garner had lived alone in a rented flat of no special quality, composed of one very large room, a bedroom, bathroom and kitchen. Zangwill, the solicitor who also acted for the local branch of the company, convened the meeting in the very large room after Miss Hayworth had served sherry and cake.

Partridge chatted here and there, smiling, eating crumbling cake and lapping up sherry. Mann looked at his watch once or twice as if anxious to get back to the office. Mrs Garner sat staring at nobody with resentment.

Zangwill began with an apology.

'It was the late Mr Garner's expressed

wish that this will should be read aloud to the — beneficiaries. I pointed out to him at the time that some of it might be — upsetting, but it was his spoken and written wish that it should be read as it is. Therefore I have no option but to continue.'

That riveted them. Silence fell, silence filled with dread, glee, greed and hope.

'Very well. This is the last will and testament . . .

' 'To my wife, Edna, who for all seven years of our marriage when we lived together, denied me sexual intercourse by every excuse, lie, pretence and subterfuge known to woman, and who finally left me for a lady of leisure, shall receive the total of the insurance taken out by me at her request during our engagement, that is, two hundred and seventy pounds, plus any interest that may have — ' '

'What!' said Mrs Garner, then went silent again, thinking that perhaps she had interrupted too soon.

' 'To my chief assistant and head buyer — ' '

'There must be something more for

me!' said Mrs Garner.

'I'm afraid not,' Zangwill said, ruefully.

'I shall contest it and say he was insane! I know he had money somewhere!'

'You must do as you think fit, Mrs Garner, of course.' Things settled down. 'May we continue? Where are we? — 'and head buyer, James Partridge, my golf clubs and my private stock of wines which is cellared for me at the Club itself, so that he may mix business with pleasure, instead of vice versa, which he has enjoyed up to now.' '

Mann blew his nose and looked as if he would burst if he let go. Rayner sat askew in his chair, holding his sherry and looking at Hagworth's legs. Miss Hayworth was looking skilfully into a wall mirror, in which she could see Rayner sprawling in his chair.

' 'To Mr Mann, my successor, I leave my office chair, which is my property, and hope that it will stay as hot for him as it was for me.

' 'To Miss Janet Hayworth, my secretary, guide and pleasure these last five years, I leave the flat in which she lives and all that it embraces, including the flat above it and all the land pertaining — ' '

'Bloody bitch,' said Mrs Garner in a hissing tone. 'Bloody incestuous whore!' She glared at Miss Hayworth.

Miss Hayworth looked at her finger-nails in calm criticism and with studied deafness.

Zangwill waited patiently, and took the opportunity to polish his glasses while Mrs Garner spoke. The others waited also, in some mental flurry of interest; Bitch they knew; whore they felt certain of, but incestuous was a new chew-over piece.

' 'Finally,' ' Zangwill, ' 'to James Elroy Rayner, whom I have admired for his instinct for single-minded survival to which he will, and probably has, put every ability and sense of dishonest representation, to himself and his affairs, I leave the rest of my estate without reserve, that is; one safe deposit box in which he will find my most prized pornographic literature, and some small items including the pair of woollen socks, with a hole in, which I asked, begged, cajoled, whined, pleaded, demanded and prayed fifty-one times for my wife to mend; these things and anything else in the box he may find in it including the key to my grandfather's case of seven cut-throat razors; this will help him to decide whether he shall continue with a life of criminal ingratitude or cut his throat.' '

Mann was on the point of apoplexy from holding his mouth and nose. Partridge was panting like a compressor pump and reddening to danger point. Miss Hayworth looked at Rayner with a quiet, speculative smile. Mrs Garner stood up.

'No sane man could have written that rubbish!' she cried. 'No sane man could have thought such things! He was insane. The will proves it!'

'But, dear Mrs Garner,' said Zangwill, 'your late husband was a successful head of a large branch of a very large business. It would be very very difficult to prove insanity when hundreds of people could say otherwise.'

Rayner was sure Mrs Garner said,

'Shit!' as she gathered up her bag and marched out, but felt he might have misheard, and laughed.

The rest of the mourners stood up and made polite preparation to get away. Rayner swallowed the rest of his sherry and then, as an aftermath, realised it was very good sherry indeed. His intent interest in the proceedings and his disturbing small undercurrents of conscience had combined to blunt his appreciation.

Miss Hayworth came up while he studied his empty glass with a faint regret.

'Have another, James,' she said, and poured while he held the glass. 'Then give me a hand clearing up.'

Zangwill came to him.

'In case you are in immediate need of some holey socks and a book at bedtime, I brought the deposit box key with me.' He laughed. 'I think the widow is downcast.'

'I think she's in battle frame,' Rayner contradicted. 'She'll fight.'

'With what chance? This is good sherry.

He was fond of his booze.' Zangwill helped himself to some more. 'How is your father? I haven't seen him lately.'

'In Australia with Mother. I have a cousin there.'

Zangwill went on to have a friendly chat with Mann; to make sure he retained his job as company adviser on a fat retaining fee, Rayner decided, as he sipped more sherry.

The others went. He took the glasses out to Miss Hayworth in the kitchen. She was washing up plates and glasses.

'You've got a block of flats,' he said. 'But I suppose you knew?'

'You've got a pair of socks,' she said. 'But I suppose you didn't know.'

'I should think a judge would have a quiet think about whether he was barmy or not, going by the will. The remarks, that is.'

'Zangwill did apologise for the grammar. Some of the sentences got lost, don't you think? But Garner enjoyed it, I'm sure. Will you give me a lift back? You've got your car.'

'Haven't you?'

'I came with the cortege, as chief organiser.'

'Yes, I'll lift you. What happens to this flat?'

'It finishes at the end of the month. The entrails go to me, but I think I'll junk it on to Edna Garner. It'll be something more for her to put up with and remind her of him.'

'You are a bitch, aren't you?' he said, with pleasure.

'What did he know about you?' she asked, taking a tray of glasses to a cupboard.

'Nothing. He just recognised a fellow bastard. Is anyone going back to the office?'

'Shouldn't think so. Pat will deal with any calls.'

'If any call can get in past her private ones.'

'I stopped that,' Miss Hayworth said. 'Everything goes through the tape now.'

'You keep all pleasures for yourself.'

'I like myself. I spoil myself — after all I've worked to deserve it.'

'You're a very good secretary. Are you

going to be as good for Mann?'

'I don't like Mann. When I don't like people, I am repulsed by my own flesh when I get near them. I'm completely self centred. I obey me. When people say I was Garner's mistress, they are damn right. I was mistress; Garner was the boy, and — do you know? — he loved it.'

She smiled and it made him angry.

'You can just catch the bank,' she said, tidying her hair in the kitchen mirror. 'It might be interesting. Bound to be amusing. He wasn't bad at ill-humour.' She laughed and turned back, taking her handbag from the dresser. 'Are you ready?'

'Any time,' he said, almost surlily.

She locked up the flat. They got in the car. She said, 'The bank?'

'Anybody'd think you were interested in my socks.'

'I don't believe it stops at socks,' she said. 'He admired you.'

'Me? You must be joking!'

'Why cliches? You can think of something better. Think rudely, nastily;

you are almost most inventive then.'

'I feel someone's been studying me,' he said sharply.

She laughed.

'Did you give him all your opinions as to my self-interest, my perfidy?'

'What I told Garner was all between me, him and the bedpost. He liked to be tied to the bedpost,' she added in calculated reminiscence.

'What?'

'Here's the bank. I'll bribe the traffic warden.'

'You're determined to poke into my — whatever he's left for my embarrassment.'

She laughed. He got out and slammed the door so the car rocked. He went in, spoke to the chief cashier and gave him the covering letter he had from Zangwill with the deposit box key. He was taken down to the strong room.

'I understand it's full of odds and ends,' he said. 'Have you a bag I could borrow?'

Of course, he could borrow anything. His father was a man of substance and dealt with the bank, and the son could certainly have a bag or anything else of no value that he wished.

He was left with a bag, the box and the key in a small cubicle like one for writing telegrams. He opened the box angrily. There were the socks, as promised, a key for the box of razors and four big flat envelopes of linen paper, each sealed with wax.

A clerk was waiting outside the steel gates looking impatient; It was near to close of business. James Elroy Rayner put all his inheritance in the bag provided, left the box and the bank.

'Socks and all?' she said.

'Socks and filthy postcards and a key for the razors — wherever they are.' He tossed the bag into the back and drove off. 'Where is this place of yours?'

She showed him. When he drove into the front garden he almost whistled.

'How in hell did he buy a place like this?' he said. 'Backing on to the river?' Suddenly he asked no more questions but stopped. 'Okay?'

'Come in. Look round,' she said. 'Might as well satisfy all your curiosity

17

at once. I'd hate you to go away wondering.'

He went in with her. It was a very nice flat indeed, on the ground floor with windows opening out onto the lawn and the river. He followed her through, trying to work out in his head how much it would have cost and how many years Garner must have fiddled the accounts to get it.

He wished he'd asked before he'd killed him.

★ ★ ★

He went back to his father's house in thoughtful mood. He stayed there while his parents were away because his father feared burglars, and because it was more comfortable than his small flat in the town. Housekeeper Mrs Colman did everything for him despite the fact that she obviously couldn't stand the sight of him. She was faithful to the family and followed their wishes.

She had every right to think him no good. He had spent much of his young life up to that time in trying to find ways of doing no good more profitably.

His plan for some years had been that the first need of a big crook is a sound background in his family, his position at his work, and in his moderate finances. With those sureties, he decided a man could carry out a carefully planned clean-up that would provide him for the remainder of his life.

Now twenty-three, he had served five years of insinuating himself into a position with a firm of considerable influence and power over that quarter of the country. Still a private organisation, it had five branches with retail outlets and a subsidiary firm manufacturing explosives and light ammunition of various kinds.

For some time he had watched Garner fiddle himself a fair slice of each weekly take by skilful adjustment of buying prices and cash which he 'lost' from the tills. It had been with the idea of catching Garner at the safe in his office, when he had gone back on his own, that Rayner had gone there and murdered him.

It had been no part of the plan to

murder. It had been a dangerous thing to do, and he was surprised to look back and realise that he had done it, and done it with a great surge of violent pleasure.

He was surprised there had been no sick reaction, but there had been no blood. Perhaps that was why.

He sat down in his father's study and shook the contents out of the borrowed bag. When he spread the envelopes out on the desk he saw they were numbered with a marker pen.

He took up a paperknife and then hesitated. It might be well to be superstitious. This was a totally unexpected gift from a man he had murdered. It was so strange that anyone in the same position might have thought the fool knew he was going to be murdered, and that this was a way of getting the last laugh.

He sat back and looked at the envelopes critically until he realised they could tell him nothing; that his hesitation was the manifestation of a murderer's nerves jangling.

He pulled the envelope 'One' towards him and very carefully broke the seal with the knife, then eased the blade along under the flap each way, until the flap was free. He lifted it and looked in.

Photographs, but they looked like colour print enlargements and he had been thinking of magazines and books. He shook out the photographs, then spread them on the desk top.

They were pornographic all right, but the photography was first class work, and seemed to have been taken against the background of a first class place, panelled corridors, rare paintings on the walls, mostly half obscured by the antics of a couple telling a brief story.

The story was very short, but with variations and embellishments, took some time to get the couple into a great hall, along a corridor and into a big kind of study where there were then scandalous goings on around the furniture.

He opened envelope 'two'. The story continued in greater detail and it was not until then that he recognised the woman in the story and sat back in astonishment.

Hagworth. Unmistakeably there was

Janet Hayworth dressed, half dressed and undressed. The dreaded Hag!

He stared at the wall a little while, then looked again with more interest. What a body she had! Because of his angry dislike of her he had fancied her assisted by long-line bras, girdles and other benefits, but his fancy had been wrong.

His astonishment faded, passed through a stage of peculiar glee and then brought up sharply in complete puzzlement.

Why on earth had Garner kept these in a safe deposit? She had been his mistress. His wife had long deserted. There had been no sensible reason at all for secrecy over the Hag at Play with some unknown boyfriend who, throughout the sequences always had his back turned somehow.

It certainly wasn't short, stocky Garner, so what was the purpose of leaving them to James Rayner? Blackmail? But why should the Hag hide anything? She wasn't married.

The puzzle was extraordinary. Suddenly he thought an answer might lie in the other two envelopes. He opened 'Three'.

A sheaf of time tables fell out, but whatever they were about was not to be known. The tops had been cut off, so only the time tables remained.

He opened 'Four'.

Ten thousand dollars in US hundred dollar bills. And that was all, but for the old socks and the key for the case of razors.

2

James Elroy Rayner sat back in his father's chair and looked at the weird inheritance spread out on the desk before him. The last wish in the last will of Henry Garner, late manager of the branch and Rayner's boss, everybody's boss — except the Hagworth, Rayner thought.

Somehow one could not imagine her being bossed by anybody, but if she ever allowed such a thing to happen, Rayner was sure it would be solely to enable her to turn it to her own advantage.

He leant forward and looked at the series of photographs, watching Miss Hayworth in each.

'She's not forty,' he said aloud. 'With that figure she couldn't be more than thirty.' He looked again. 'Perhaps even less. The bitch.'

He pushed the prints away with an

irritated gesture. A gong began to ring in the hall. Mrs Colman, his parents' housekeeper preferred the gong to announce his meals. She was obviously unwilling to talk to James Elroy unless there was no other way.

'Just coming!' he called out.

Carefully he put the various articles back into their original envelopes, and put the lot in the lower drawer of the desk.

Hagworth reveals all, a pair of worn-out socks, a few time tables and ten thousand dollars.

As he went out into the dining room he wondered what possible connection there could be between this array of oddities that would fit in with the late Garner's twisted sense of humour.

The ten thousand dollars, which an ordinary person would have been pleased about, was tainted in Rayner's mind because it had been left by Garner.

The first thing he thought was that the notes were forgeries, but how to tell for certain? He did not fancy going into his bank and asking. It might turn out to be some obscene joke that would explode in his face if he did.

If they were forgeries, they were useless. So were time tables which had no titles. So were worn out socks and a key to a case which might be anywhere in the whole wide world. And so, perhaps, were pictures of Hagworth, however arresting.

He ate without interest, and infested with a fog of curious problems he found himself turning his mental energy back and wondering how old the woman really was.

That annoyed him, as if he had become aware the pictures were getting into him.

Perhaps that was Garner's intention, knowing how much Rayner hated the woman. Perhaps that was just it; to bring her to his mind in the most grabbing way he could imagine.

Obviously, Garner had found the prints precious, but why had he kept them in a bank vault? He had been, to all intents and purposes, a bachelor able to please himself.

So there was no reason why he should

have hidden the pictures in such a way, as they had no intrinsic value.

Then uneasiness began to creep into his mind from quite another direction. The weird collection of effects had been thought up specially for him.

And placed in a bank vault to make a joke after his death.

But what had given Garner the idea he would die?

He left the meal unfinished and looked at the ornate light fitting hanging over the table.

When had the will been written? It must have been very recently, because before that it would not have been possible to know that Mann would succeed him if and when he retired.

In fact the whole thing had been astonishingly up to date.

The cold shock he felt made his mind recoil from going along that path. If he didn't hold back he would soon, like Macbeth, be seeing the ghost of his victim joining him at dinner one night.

Of course, it was only natural that he should feel strained about it all, but not over Garner. Garner was dead and buried. Garner had died last Thursday night and had been buried today, Wednesday. The inquest had been slotted in with three others so that the coroner had not been long kept from his more remunerative occupation.

'You were passing the office building and saw the light still shining, Mr Rayner?'

'Yes. That was getting on for midnight. I thought I had better look in, just to make sure everything was all right. A lot of cash was left there over Thursday nights.'

'Yes; so we have already heard, Mr Rayner.'

'The main office door was locked, but I have a key. I went in and found him in his office lying on the carpet by the safe. The safe was open and money was inside.'

'Yes, yes, yes, yes, yes, yes, accidental death. Next? Next, next, next . . . '

He saw it over again, the mortuary-like little room, and old Pheesome nattering like some sort of impatient bird. How did such people keep such jobs?

He shrugged and got up. Mrs Colman walked in. She didn't ask if he'd finished, just looked at the table, and began clearing it.

'Didn't like it? Well, please yourself — ' She did not talk to him but to the table.

He left her to it and walked out and up to his room. He washed and changed, out of his funeral garb. Looking in the mirror to tie his bow he seemed to feel his sight growing outwards beyond the glass, and he was again standing at the graveside watching Hagworth across the open grave. He felt uneasy, and wished she would lift the veil so he could see her eyes. He knew they were watching him but could not tell for sure.

He felt a sudden rage against her for not lifting the veil so he could see her eyes. She stood there in the fine tailored black suit, watching him, but he could not see her eyes. Suddenly he saw her standing naked there, like the prints, but still with the hat on and the veil hiding her thoughts.

He turned away, put on a jacket, went downstairs and out to the car. He drove to The Horns, by the river. The bar was quite full. A meeting of the Rowing Club had just ended. He was surprised it was so late. He wondered what on earth he had been doing to let the time pass like that.

Barman Harry said, 'Good funeral?'

'It disposed of the matter,' Rayner said.

The barman laughed and got his drink. Rayner paid.

'Left you a fortune, I suppose?' the barman said.

'Ten thousand dollars,' said Rayner before he was sorry for having said it.

'Ha! I bet and all,' said the barman. 'My grandpa used to sing some old music hall song about Ten Thousand Stand-Up Collars. About some chap on a desert island, shipwrecked — Good evening! Yes, sir? Your pleasure?' He flounced away talking all the time to various people round the bar, getting drinks, taking money, ringing the till, and talking.

It jangled on Rayner like the ringing of the till. Somehow when the drawer shot out he saw the open safe again.

The Topical Will. Had Garner had some idea he would die? How could he? Or had he been thinking of doing himself in? Suicide? Why? He hadn't been found out. He was in with the Hagworth, he had money —

No, he hadn't had money. It had gone into the property he had left her. Funny sort of thing to do, come to think of it. Put everything into the property and leave no cash for expenses. Of course, it would keep the property out of the hands of the widow, because that would have been in the Hagworth's name, for certain.

'How was the old ashes to ashes syndrome?' Auctioneer Freddy Jarvis sat down on the stool beside him.

'Dusty,' said Rayner. 'Good market today?'

'So-so. Sheep and pigs mostly. Only a few cows. Have you got the Garner job?'

'Me? I'm dogsbody.'

'Oh, it wasn't worth murdering him for, then?' he laughed.

'What do you mean?' Rayner said coldly.

'Macbeth. Murder 'em all, one by one, till you're king, but have no subjects. They're all dead. See it Sunday? On the box.'

'I did — part of it,' Rayner said, faintly surprised that that must have been where the Banquo thought had come from. 'Avaunt and quit my sight! Avaunt! — there was a time the man was dead, the brains were out, and there an end — ' How did it go?

'What's the matter lad? Swallowed a bee?'

'I was trying to remember my Shakespeare.'

'I've been trying. Funny. I enjoyed it on the box, and hated it at school. They made me play Titania once. I was so ashamed and didn't know what about. They confuse kids, you know. How's that Miss Hayworth or Hayward? Was she there? I could do her a bit of good.'

'She has a face like a lost bus.'

'Faces don't matter. Hell! is that the time? Come back and have a drink, lad. That'll stop the wife nagging me. The Rowing Club's not on with her. She thinks we fill the bloody boats with beer.'

Rayner agreed. The wife's nagging was merely postponed. When Freddy walked his friend into the split-level lounge Freda was watching television in her nightgown and slippers and without looking round she said, 'That bloody central heating's too high.'

Then she saw the guest and said something else.

'Haven't you got a dressing gown, for Sod's sake?' said Freddie.

'It's over the chair there.' She pointed. 'Chuck it.'

Freddy chucked it so that it landed over her head and fell round her like a tent. Being tight he called out, 'Catch!' far too late. Everything he did appeared, to Rayner, to guarantee Freddie would be nagged all night.

Slowly Freda pulled the gown off her tousled head. She stood up and put the gown on. Her annoyance at being interrupted in her enjoyment of the play, by a drunken husband and a friend, brought in as a defence ploy, showed in the stiff line of her body as she moved.

'I brought Jim,' said Freddy, lamely. 'He's been at a funeral all day. Poor chap.'

She looked at Rayner, who made a slight, comical gesture of helplessness.

'Find yourself a seat, Jim,' she said. 'You'd like a drink. I'm sure. So would I. Freddy seems to have had his share already.'

'Here, I say, girl!' His protest faded into a mumble and he laughed, painfully. 'Don't move. I'll get them, don't move.'

'Whose funeral?' she said, turning to Rayner.

Rayner told her.

'Oh, that one,' she said. 'There's a buzz going round it was really a murder but it went wrong somehow and the thief panicked and got out.'

'Where did you hear that?' he said, showing a mild interest.

'Oh, it's just sort of general gossip,'

she said. 'It's only a small town, after all. What else do they have to talk about?' She laughed, and took her drink from Freddie without looking at him.

Curiously the rumour had not come his way.

He wondered, with a slight tightening of the nerves, if the gossipers had not cared to mention it to him.

* * *

She shook her head before she spoke again.

'It's not possible?' she said.

'Well, the door was locked when I went up there,' he said. 'Furthermore, the amount of cash in the safe tallied with the takings, so what would be the motive?'

'I don't know. It's just one of those things people like to have guesses at, specially when it happens round the corner. Perhaps somebody didn't like him?'

'Managers are not generally popular,' he said, with a smile. 'It's the breed. But you don't murder them.'

'No, I don't, personally. Was there a woman in the case somewhere?'

'I wouldn't know about his private life,' Rayner said, but by tomorrow everybody would know Garner had left his property to Miss Hayworth. 'Though he did leave a flat to his secretary.'

'Miss Hayworth?' said Freddie, suddenly interested.

'Oh?' said Freda, frigidly, and turned her head to the Guilty Man. 'Do you know Miss Hayworth?'

'Oh — yes, yes — in a way,' he said, passing it off with unnecessary carelessness. 'We did the sale of that place. She was the tenant.'

'Oh,' said Freda with cold interest, 'she paid him rent?'

'One assumes — ' said Freddie, and laughed briefly. 'One can't actually assume the worst — or the best — as you see fit — ' He laughed again but stopped when he saw her watching him.

'What's she like?' Freda said.

'Ugly,' said Rayner. 'Overbearing by nature.'

Freda turned to him. 'But she's efficient, I suppose?'

'Oh yes. Strictly.'

'She can't be very ugly if the man left her a flat.'

'Each to his own gout, as the French say!' Freddie was about to laugh loudly at his wit, but then thought the time, and the joke, not fitting.

Rayner thought that if he felt so trampled by his wife, he ought to trample back or walk out. But perhaps she had something far more than beer at the Rowing Club held against him. Perhaps she had found out about a girl on the side, or something like that which rankled strongly.

Thinking of the pair took his mind off the Hagworth.

The shock that gave him, when he realised it, made him grip his glass with a sudden tightening of the fingers.

The proper order of his thoughts should have been; Murder Gossip, first, and details trailing from it, second. Instead the Hagworth had come to mind first.

What was the matter with him? Did he, at the back of his mind, have the idea that she *knew* what had happened that night?

'I've never heard about a secretary before,' Freda said. 'That's rather odd. In the gossip, I mean. People who like gossip and start guessing at a murder usually turn to finding some reason next, and they like a woman for a reason best of all.'

'They will probably think of it when they hear about the flat,' said Rayner, sarcastically.

'Well, yes, I should think they would. Another gin, Freddie, if you please.'

'Of course, dear! Sit there — ' He jumped up, took her glass and turned to the table. 'But the tenancy was all above board, I may say, and I know old Garner's wife left him donkey's years ago, so he wouldn't want to leave her anything if he could help it.'

'She is his wife, you said?' said Freda, cold again.

'Well, yes, darling, but — she hoofed it years ago — with another woman,

to boot. Not the sort of thing a chap
— likes — '

'No, a chap would prefer a woman
to run away with another chap and a
chap to run away with another woman?'
Freda said.

'Well, I mean — something in order,
you know what I mean. Sort of two-by-
two idea. You know?'

By this time Rayner was convinced
Freddy had been found out in a matter of
extra-marital indiscretion, and that Freda
could see a fur coat, a new car and a few
other things in the discovery. He was glad
he had not married.

'I can never see that a lover can be
worth murdering for,' said Freda, turning
back to Rayner. 'Can you, Jim?'

'Frankly, no. But it's a way of life for
some. Love of self is very melodramatic.'

From the corner of his eye he saw
Freddy knocking back a large Scotch
while holding his wife's refilled glass in
his other hand. His back was turned to
her, of course.

What a life, Rayner thought. Being
watched, being suspected, being sat on

for something which he might well have stopped doing by the time he was found out. So Freddy would have lost his mistress and the favours of his wife. It was a terrible punishment.

Rayner wanted to laugh. Freddie came and took his glass to refill. When he did so, Rayner saw he downed another large Scotch with his back turned to Freda.

It was an almost unbearable domestic scene to witness. Rayner was beginning to enjoy it and Freddy gave him his glass with some lack of aim. Sensing this himself, Freddy turned away with more than ordinary precision, staggered and began to topple sideways. To save himself he tottered in a crablike manner and thumped against the door with a crash that made Freda almost spill her drink.

'Fred!' she cried. 'Go to bed! Go up to your room! Up!'

Poor Fred leant against the door, uncertain as to what had actually happened and what would be best done next. His body moved in a slightly sinuous motion as he leaned against the door, as if steadying himself against the swinging of the room.

'Okay — okay, shut your bloody trap — I'm going — '

He could not find the handle. The quick stiff Scotches had completed the joy amassed at the Rowing Club. He was almost incapable.

Freda got up, strode purposefully to the door, held his arm firmly to stop him rolling away, then, as he stood back slightly, she opened the door and pushed him through.

'Okay okay — thanks!' he bawled before Freda slammed the door.

Rayner stood up and put his glass down. She came back.

'No, don't go,' she said.

They heard him crash and thump his way up the stairs. She sighed, looked at Rayner and shrugged.

'Sorry, Jim,' she said.

Somehow his mind put the Hagworth in her place and he was making her say 'Sorry' and it roused a kind of satisfied fury in him. He put a hand on her shoulder and gripped. She looked at him.

41

She let him turn her to him.

Upstairs the thumping went on erratically.

He pushed her quite strongly backwards on to the sofa.

A solitary thump sounded above, and then no more.

* * *

Freda got some drinks.

'I'm surprised,' she said, and laughed quietly.

He said nothing. He could not sort out his thoughts, or get the Hagworth out of them. It had to be the suspicion that she *knew*.

He took the drink from Freda and smiled.

'I think I had the idea before,' he said.

'Yes, I should imagine you did. You were quite ferocious.'

He wanted to leave, but his subconscious mind seemed to say there was safety in hanging on a while.

Then Freddy fell out of bed. There was a crash that threatened to bring down part of the ceiling. She swore and put her drink down.

'You'd better go, sweetie.' She kissed him.

He saw her go upstairs and then left. He drove slowly home. It was a clear moonlit night. The talk about murder worried him. Gossip, yes; there was bound to be gossip, possibly starting with a joke, like 'I wouldn't put it past that lot to do him in, eh? Ha, ha!' And going on from there.

But jokes often turned slowly into something else, specially when the subject of the joke was attractive, or exciting. Murder was both, and chilling too, when it might have happened in the next street.

He turned into the drive and stopped. The hall lights were on. Mrs Colman always left them on when she went. It kept away burglars, she sometimes said.

As he went in, the grandfather clock struck. He looked at the ornate face. Half past one, and he was restless. He went into the kitchen, got milk and drank it. Being thirsty was caused by nervous tension. He had nervous tension. Guilt had come to life that day, perhaps at the reading of the will. Perhaps at the finding of ten thousand dollars.

No. It had started to move inside him when that bloody woman had watched him from behind her veil, looking across the grave which his handiwork had dug for Garner.

But surely, she wouldn't kick? She had what she wanted sooner than she could have expected. Lucky old Hagworth. Bloody old Hagworth.

He went back into his father's study, sat down at the desk and got the envelopes out of the drawer. He shook out the photographs and spread them so they made a continuous strip.

He looked through them quickly, so that the figures almost seemed to move through that great hall, along a corridor and into the big room with the heavy furniture.

He saw all that, then realised he was watching the woman all the time, concentrating on her.

What the hell was the point?

He sat back and tried to see some reason in the prints, but he could find nothing to start on. Then something occurred.

The hair-do. It was short and with a shark's tooth fringe.

That had not been so long ago. He remembered her coming in for the first time like it, and the staff passing quiet remarks behind her back, because before that she had worn it straight and long, so that the change was most noticeable.

Since that time, while the hair was growing again, she had a smart hair do with a bun of her own hair pinned at the back.

Then the hair cut must have been last summer; late last summer, about eight months before.

Then he remembered the hot September when the girls had been sunbathing on the flat roof at lunch times.

That was when Pat had said, 'She's tanned all over. No patches. Made me envious.'

It was beginning to come back. He got a glass of Scotch and studied the prints again in case there could be some other details that might help.

The earrings. Big pearls. He thought she had had those a long time because he had seen them with her long hair showing the pearls now and again as she turned her head.

He sat back again and felt uneasy that his endeavours to place the date were making him think too much, too closely, of her.

The dollars. The time tables. He got out the tables and looked at them again. They looked like bus tables. There were no little footnote marks for dining cars, sleepers and other details applicable to trains.

Bus tables, but what system and where? The titles had been cut off and the destination names down the left hand side had gone, too.

Identifying those might take weeks of looking at other bus tables and then comparing. He tipped out the dollars and sorted them through carefully, in case any scrap of paper had been left in between. There was nothing.

He sat back then and looked at the prints.

Last September, but where? And why?

He got up angrily. All the damned things were doing was to keep her in his mind as a sort of major clue to all the other things he wanted to know.

He hated that as he hated her.

3

The next morning he spoke to Pat Browne who was in charge of the office girls, telephones, personal records and general odds and ends. She was blonde, twenty-five, married, waiting for a divorce and given to laughing inexplicably and trying to stifle it when people asked the reason.

'A personal question from the files,' Rayner said, putting on conspiratorial charm.

'Ask away, Lothario. I've only a dozen and one things to do at once or sooner.'

'How old *is* the Hagworth?'

'What a pity,' she said. 'That'll spoil all the guessing. I'll just make sure, but I think she's thirty.'

She went to the personal file cabinet and made sure. She closed it again and nodded.

'Thirty last November twelfth. She seems older because she knows the World and how to deal with it.' She slammed the drawer shut. 'Why the sudden interest?'

'You haven't seen the local paper?'

'Mr Mann's got it.'

'Old Garner left her a block of flats, including the one she lives in. When the will was read the wife went mad and had to be carried out in a straitjacket.'

'That doesn't surprise me. The flats, I mean. I knew Garner was having it off with her, but then I wasn't sure it wasn't just one of her passing fancies.'

'One of?' He was surprised and interested.

'Oh, yes. There were several. I just happen to know, but girls stick together in some things where it isn't dead personal. Like rivalry, I mean. But if he left her a flat — well, that changes things a bit. Makes it public. That's what roused your houndlike nose, was it?'

'And yours.'

'Well, it's rather exciting in a backhanded sort of way.'

Partridge came in to get to his own office.

'Morning, sweetness. Hallo, Rayner.

How are you getting on with the burnt-out socks?' He laughed and went into his office.

'Burnt-out socks?' said Pat, wondering.

Rayner explained. She laughed. He reckoned the socks would keep her laughing all day.

'Dirty postcards, a key to a box that isn't there and a pair of burnt-out socks,' she said, big-eyed. 'Why, darling, its absolutely *you!*'

He left her shaking with laughter and went into his small office. Mann came in with the local paper in his hand.

'Cartwright's man's coming over this morning sometime, about that reject stuff that got in amongst the last load. Fix him for complete replacement plus five percent off another full load.'

'That is hard,' Rayner said, eyes brightening.

'It's business. One must catch the advantage when it presents itself.'

'Especially when one is new in the seat,' said Rayner, smiling.

Mann stared curiously.

'Didn't Garner screw them?'

'Oh yes, when he could,' said Rayner, and to himself he added, 'But it didn't go in the books.'

Mann put the paper on the desk.

'Seen this?'

'Yes. At home. They've made it all Miss Hayworth. That'll start the tongues in chorus.'

'Well, he doesn't care, and I don't think she will.'

'I'll show it to her. She may not have seen it.'

'Sadist.'

'Not at all. Sentimentalist. She'll enjoy it.'

Mann went into his office. Rayner went into the secretary's room next door to his and which had a door into the manager's office.

She was reading through some letters and smoking a cigarette. She looked up when he came in. For some reason her dark, shining hair with the bun pinned on the back of her head fascinated him, as if he had touched it and the feel had given him some weird excitement.

'The rag's given you a puff,' he said,

and put the paper down on her desk. He watched her read it.

She smiled and shrugged, then pushed the paper back across the desk.

'Pity they didn't have a picture to put in,' he said, and felt irritated because he had said it.

'Yes.' She looked up with those calm, steady eyes. 'I take a good photograph. In a veil.'

That was a killer. Again he was surprised, but this time because her remark killed any ability he had to reply. He could not think of anything. She was beating him, and she was pleasantly aware of it.

'Your paper,' she said, as he turned to go.

'It's the office copy,' he said, and went.

She smiled at his back.

★ ★ ★

At the High Street offices of Jarvis & Trant, Freddie Jarvis was bright, red-faced, energetic and apparently unaffected by the illness caught at the Rowing Club meeting.

'Let's have the file on Trellis Court, Jessie,' he told his secretary. 'There's been a change of ownership.'

'I saw that in the News,' Jessie said, smiling understandingly. 'I'll bring it in to you.'

'No, let's have it now, Jess,' he said, and stood by her at the filing cabinet and stroked her behind while she concentrated on finding the file.

'There, Freddy.'

'I kiss your hand,' he said, and did. He took the file into his office. He looked through it quickly then rang for Jessie to come in. 'That top flat being empty, I wonder if she'll want to sell it?'

'She may let it for a while,' Jessie said, demure as a soft, charming country girl should be. 'I don't think she'll sell anything — not for a while.'

'A while? You mean a decent interval,' he said, and laughed. 'Have you heard any — sort of, gossip?'

'Well, of course. But there always is gossip in this place.'

'If there'd been a murder the police would have spotted it. They're not fools. Besides, the bloody place was locked on the inside when Jim found it. The man just fell on the safe and cracked his noggin. It's easily done, after you've been working all day.'

'If somebody had a key, though,' she said, thoughtfully.

'What — one of the staff?' He sat upright, his eyes bulging. 'You don't mean *her?*'

'I don't. I don't think she'd be so stupid, specially as she must have known she was to get all that out of it, and anyhow, she had it before he was dead, as good as, so why take risks?'

'That's a very shrewd view, Jessie. Very shrewd. Yes, she did have the place, anyhow. In fact she had the lot. I wonder why he didn't let the top flat again after the Bolson crowd moved out?'

'Perhaps she didn't like anybody watching her affairs,' said Jessie, beautifully calm. 'By the way, Alice is doing yesterday's accounts. Farmer Weston's credit is getting very large.'

'He's all right,' he said, quickly, 'but I'll look in there sometime and wedge the cheque book from under his pants. He's got a persecution mania over bills.'

She made a squiggle in her knee book. She said nothing more about Farmer Weston, but she didn't approve of some old friends having credit and poorer dogs having none.

'Anything else come to mind?'

'The auction down at the Hall tomorrow,' she said. 'Bill Evitt's lost his licence and can't move all that furniture and stuff, so I booked Gillow to do it. That all right?'

'Can't stand the bastard, but needs must, I suppose. Poor old Bill. What's he going to do then? We'll have to fix him up with something. Something in the market, perhaps. Or can he get another driver?'

'His bank says no.'

'We'll think of something. Ask him to drop in. What shall I do about the heiress Hayworth?'

'Well, everybody's dropping in, so why

not drop in this evening, and crawl away afterwards?' She rose, smiling quietly, as usual.

'You women,' he sighed. 'All right. Back to your cave. I'll send in a leg of toad, but a sailor's thumb might be a bit more difficult.'

'Darling,' she said, as the door opened behind her.

Freda walked in, confident, buoyant, sparkling, conquering, spring coat swinging open, handbag held to her side like a hip gun.

'Hallo, Jessie,' she said, sweetly. 'Busy?'

'Very, Mrs Jarvis,' said Jessie, and went, smiling softly.

'Freddy, my own, I want to spend some money but not mine,' Freda said, with joyful certainty of success. 'Give me a cheque.'

He hesitated. 'How much?' he said.

'Leave it open,' she said.

He pulled out his book from a drawer and signed one cheque.

'What have I done?' he said, gloomily.

'Nothing, darling. I just thought you'd like to give your ever loving, lovely, ever faithful wife a present.' She smiled brilliantly.

'Of course,' he said, still gloomy and tearing the paper very slowly as if frightened of hurting it. 'What time did Jim go?' He looked up as he handed her the cheque.

'Just after you staggered to rest,' she said, folding the spoils.

'Good chap, old Jim,' said Freddy. 'He never minds.'

She looked at him, then bent and kissed his cheek.

'I may be late,' she said, and went.

'What the hell did I do?' he muttered, staring at the closed door.

Something reminded him of Jim and his going into the office that night, then finding the manager all dead and bloody on the floor.

'Enough to spoil the beer,' he said, and got on with his work.

Freda walked to the firm's bank and got her money. Then she went to a phone box and rang through to Pat.

'He's engaged just at the moment,' Pat said.

'I won't keep him,' Freda said.

'I'll put you through.'

Rayner said, 'Yes?'

'I want to see you this evening, Jimmy. I shall be at the Park entrance, river side, at six.'

'I'll see to that,' Rayner said, after a pause.

He finished his interview tersely, and the man from Cartwright's was not pleased. Rayner realised he had made an error in losing his temper, but the man from Cartwright's went, leaving the impression that something would arrive as a result of his sudden going.

He was standing by his desk when the Hagworth came in.

'Before you go to lunch — oh, has he gone?' She looked round in surprise.

'Yes.'

She turned back to him.

'I want to see you this evening,' she said. 'It is about our private business.'

He felt a coldness in his stomach.

'I have an appointment this evening,' he said, shortly.

'Cancel. Come to my flat at eight.

There are some matters which need to be discussed.' She smiled quietly, but to herself.

He watched her walk back to her own office and did nothing. He stood for some minutes looking out of the window at the gathering green of the trees in the Park.

Something was going wrong, and it was taking him by surprise. The call from Freda had been so unexpected it had been a shock. Her reaction — overbearing, as it seemed to him — was something he had not come across before.

'I want to see you . . . I *want* to see you . . . ' As if he were not to be consulted, only to be told.

Yet, when he thought of defying the order, something cold gripped his inside; as if the thought of opposing someone had suddenly given him fear.

What was he frightened of in Freda?

Hagworth he could understand. He had always had a wariness about her because of her weird efficiency, and the way she seemed to see through people.

Somehow she knew he had murdered

Garner and was quite satisfied that he had done it, but for some reason, wished to cover herself.

Or *was* that it?

Had he always known she would know, that when it eventually happened, he had done it?

He turned suddenly and went out of his office. Pat looked up from her desk.

'I'll be back after lunch,' he said.

She watched him go and wondered what had gone wrong. She could smell a sudden Wrong atmosphere, she always said, and kept quiet when she did.

★ ★ ★

A succession of callers came into his office during the afternoon. Mann came in four times with queries, sheafs of papers in his hand, asking him to take over things he had never had to deal with before. Partridge came in tight, more affable than ever, and when he perceived Rayner's short temper went back on his old foolish teasing.

'What you need is a quiet afternoon

on the Hagworth, boy. That'll cool you down, my lad.'

'Get out!'

'Ah, two afternoons at least,' Partridge said, going to the door. 'She'd probably kill you, seeing what she got out of the dear, departed Garner.'

He went. The phone directory hit the door as he shut it.

'Stupid bastard!' Rayner muttered.

He left the office at half past five and had a drink at the pub just along the road. He went back, got his car and drove slowly through the Park to the river gate.

He did not see her, but there were three cars parked along the road on either side of the gate with people waiting in them.

He stopped, got out and left the car. A woman in a small car raised a hand briefly. He went towards it, his heart beating fast, though why he did not know.

The ghost of Banquo was beginning to walk.

He grinned unpleasantly as the Banquo

thought came into his mind and lurked there like the ghost itself awaiting its cue.

As he came to the small car the woman leant across and opened the door. He got in.

'What's the matter?' he said.

She stared in surprise.

'What's the matter?' She paused in a hurt astonishment that began to turn to anger. 'Didn't you do me last night, or did I dream it? What's the *matter*? Hell, I felt like seeing you! What do you take me for? A one night stand?'

He could see she was hurt, and furious. Freddy crawled about on the carpet when she was furious, and by now he must have found out this was best.

But Rayner didn't have to do that. At the same time, he felt he shouldn't make enemies. Not women enemies. They were not predictable. They seemed able to let everything go in a blaze of fury. Not like a man; a man would hold back something in case of defeat; leave an escape route by keeping other people out of the row.

He pulled himself together.

'I'm sorry, Freda,' he said, putting a hand on her arm. 'You sounded so terse this morning I thought perhaps something had gone wrong.'

'What are you nervous about?' She watched him. 'Nerves? That's new for you, isn't it?'

Words came into his head and frightened him that they might come out, no matter how he tried to stop them. They know about me. The woman knows about me. Garner knew about me. You are beginning to know about me.

'I've had a load of trouble today. Everything went wrong, and it's not over yet. I've got an appointment at eight to try and sort out part of it. There could be a lot of trouble in it for me.'

'Tonight?' she said stiffly.

Again he put his hand on her arm.

'Let's go along the river, have a quiet drink. I'll take you to dinner tomorrow.'

'Not tomorrow,' she said. 'I can't be out every bloody evening.'

'I'm sorry, really. But you took me by surprise.'

'So did you me.' She laughed as if her temper was subsiding. 'Take your car and lead. I'll follow. It'll be locked in the park, otherwise. And it'll be better, anyhow.'

'Of course.' He got out and went back to his car.

She didn't want to be found out. Perhaps she hadn't had an affair since marrying Freddy, or was just prudent. Either way, her attitude suited him. He felt almost relieved at discovering her caution.

'I hope the silly cow hasn't fallen, or something absurd,' he murmured as he started up, and a new angle of apprehension started up with the engine.

He took the lead and saw that she followed a way behind. Some traffic eased between them. He began to lose her and slowed, then saw her again, way back. He waited, going slower. Two more cars passed her and he signalled for them to overtake him. They went by.

He saw the little car turn off the road, and go out of sight. She had changed her mind.

He went on to the pub by himself, had two drinks and felt less anxious about his position. Now and again he looked round the bar, but it was not a pub he used more than very occasionally and he was not known there, nor did he see anyone he knew.

After looking a second time at one man further down the bar, he realised, with faint surprise, that there was no reason in hell why he should care if anyone saw him there. He was alone. He could go where he liked.

He began to get a feeling that he was living in a world of shadows with human shapes which gathered around him, gestured and intimidated, but which had no more existence than a passing thought in his head.

To hell with Banquo! This ghost was Hagworth's child. She was the reason these wavering images were touching his nerves. She and the way she had of seeming to *know*.

He left his second drink unfinished and went out. He drove to the flats. It was seven fifteen.

There was no answer when he pressed the ground floor bell. The delay dampened his resolution to confront her at a time of his own choosing.

He looked back at the car, then turned and pressed the bell again.

Nothing happened. He went away to wait. Somehow she always won. Everything happened her way. He had to wait and strain to wonder what it was she wanted, and he would get edgy with waiting.

Perhaps she was in all the time. Probably. She was just playing the stress game with him.

He drove along the river bank lane and stopped by the grass which ran down to the bank. A practice eight went smoothly by in its arrowlike boat, cutting along the middle of the river, the cox's voice faint and pleasant on the warm air of early evening.

There was gold edging the fresh young green of the trees and the river was calm.

What could be wrong in a world like this? Why had this odd depression come to him during that day? The women; one after the other, unexpectedly demanding.

But what was wrong, now he came to think. There was nothing that had not been there all the time to go wrong. Freda had not been expected, but, probably, Freda was safe. She wouldn't blow it.

What did it matter if she did? Only that, at this time, he did not want to get involved in any gossip. Gossip was a catching sort of habit; once it caught one person, it tended to keep on at him, tie more and more bits to his tail.

He certainly didn't want that. He didn't want Freddy getting mad, either. Freddy could pull strings and get the ear of people who might begin to wonder . . .

His anger rose again at the dreary insistence of Depression keeping on at him, like some sort of shark that wouldn't stay in the pool but kept trying to get at him. He kept smacking it back with the flat of an oar — Like Macbeth smacking away at Banquo's ghost with a huge wide paddle-like oar —

He got out of the car and walked slowly up and down on the grass. He was imagining things, odd things, odd corners of the world that had lain dormant in his mind before.

He was beginning to haunt himself with fears that Janet Hayworth had brought to life by staring at him across the open grave —

He got back in the car and slammed the door. The clock showed seven forty-three. Strain. Stress. Stretching the minutes out so that he could not believe so little time had passed on the clock face.

He turned on the radio, pushed buttons but found nothing that brought quiet and interest to his head. He watched a girl walking along the towpath, the quick smartness of her heels making her breasts shake.

He could wait until she passed, then jump out and grab her from behind, a hand over her mouth the other twisting her arm up behind her back, feel her taut, quivering body against his, rigid with shock and fear —

Then he could let her go and say, 'Oh, I'm so sorry; I thought it was my mother,' and watch her run away.

But she would go to the police. He didn't want that. He watched her pass, then jerked his head to the front.

His fingers tapped the wheel. He could see the nerve strings in them taut and straining, crabbing them like claws with the tension of waiting.

Her cold voice spoke again in the quiet of the car, saying, 'I want to see you this evening, about our private business.'

What private business was there? None. He knew of none. He should have asked her what she meant, but he hadn't.

Why hadn't he asked? Why hadn't he done the very thing that would have stopped this tension? Why had he stood there and by doing nothing, caused the very thing that had tortured him ever since? The very thing he had known at the time would have this very result?

He started up and turned the car, back towards the flats.

4

He rang the bell. Once more nothing happened. He looked back at his car on the drive and the lawn beyond running to the bushes barring the grounds from the road. It was getting dusky in the distance beyond the trees.

He rang again, angrily this time and kept his finger on the bell for several seconds. He heard nothing when he released it.

Perhaps the bloody woman wasn't in. Perhaps she'd forgotten. How could she forget? Didn't it matter? Private business, hadn't she said? Something like that? Or was it some kind of joke?

But she didn't joke like that. He didn't think she could joke any way. And yet —

Private business. *Our* private business. What was it? Had he taken something meaningless as a threat, and so given himself away to her? Suppose she was inside, just letting him ring and ring, and laughing while he rang? Suppose she was in there laughing at his stupid revelation of guilt?

He turned to go back to his car when another came in to the drive from the road. It was not hers — unless she had bought another that day. He waited on the step, then suddenly he recognised the car's driver.

'Freddy,' he said, as the car stopped. He was surprised, but then the idea came that Freddy might have had some sort of appointment with the Hagworth. Partridge's continued jibing at him for not seeing the Hagworth as Sexpot nudged his mind as Freddy gazed out of the window.

'She isn't in,' Rayner said, coming down the steps.

'Oh well,' Freddy sighed. 'It was just on an offchance. Wanted to see if she was going to do anything about selling the upstairs flat.'

'She rang me about some business that has turned up,' Rayner said. 'But she isn't here.' He shrugged.

'Bit odd for her, isn't it?' Freddy said, raising his bushy eyebrows. 'Not the forgetful sort, I shouldn't have thought.'

'Oh something might have happened to hold her up.' Rayner turned to his car. 'I'll leave it, anyhow. She can ring again if things are that grotty.'

'Come back for a drink?' Freddy said, hopefully.

'No, thanks, Fred. Not tonight. You poured that Scotch a mite too heavy last night.' He grinned and went to his car.

They passed each other with a wave and set off in their opposite directions. Rayner drove back to his father's house. The Hagworth's empty car was standing outside. He drove in through the gate and to the garage beside the house. As he walked to the front door his inside was taut with anger that had a quiver of fear vibrating in it.

It was then eight fifteen, and Mrs Colman would have gone. She always left at 7.45 whether he was in or not, leaving instructions as to his food.

He used his key. The hall was empty, and he heard nothing. All the room doors

72

were shut. Mrs Colman shut all doors when she went 'in case of fire'.

'Miss Hayworth!'

Even as he called, the study door opened and she stood there.

'It was necessary to change our arrangement,' she said. 'I tried to reach you.'

He could see past her and saw that the photographs from the first and second envelopes were spread out on the desk top.

'You've been through the desk,' he said, furiously.

'You surely don't think that legacy was meant entirely for you, do you?' she said with maddening assurance.

'I don't know why I was left them at all,' he said, sourly. 'Starting at the beginning, why were they taken? Secondly, why did he keep them locked up?'

'They were taken because he paid,' she said, calmly. 'He employed the man and the photographer with his lighting girl, and arranged to hire the house. It was all very professional.'

He looked at them again.

'I did a lot of that kind of modelling at one time,' she went on. 'They used my shape and stuck on another girl's face. You couldn't see the joins. It was while I was doing that work I met Mr Garner.'

He was startled.

'A long time back?'

'Ten years. Just over.'

'Before you went into the firm?'

'Oh yes. Garner arranged all that. He was a clever arranger. Everything had a purpose, though it wasn't at all obvious.'

He looked up.

'What was our private business?' he said.

'This.' She indicated the desk top. 'I guessed these were the pictures mentioned in the will, and I never saw the finished product.' She smiled slowly. 'Nor did I ever know the meaning behind them.'

He began to feel his anger turning against himself. He could not look at her while those prints were on the desk.

She was making a boy out of him.

'What meaning?' he snapped.

'No need to shout, James. Everything he did had a meaning. He never spent money without some reason for doing it, usually gain.' She looked at him. 'You are embarrassed. Don't be a fool. His private life was dedicated to creating embarrassment for others. Don't let him laugh in his damned grave.'

'I say again; what meaning?'

'This display cost him a lot in outlay,' she said, waving a hand over it. 'We went to the place by hired helicopter, with these professionals, and that represented a lot of money. He said he had sold some shares at the right time.'

'And you didn't think this was all a bit downgrade?'

'For him? No. He liked that kind of thing. After all, what is it? Something if you like it, nothing if you don't.'

'You were his mistress. What was the need?'

She laughed.

'The need is what I want to find out. He loved making mysteries. But some he made because he didn't want anyone outside to understand what he meant. This is obviously one of those.'

'Then why leave it to me?'

'You forget. You have it only because he died. He didn't think he would die.' She looked at him calmly.

'Who does?' he said and looked at her at last. Her eyes seemed to hold his with a lazy certainty in the greenish lenses. 'Eyes like a bloody cat,' he said angrily.

She laughed.

'Keep to the subject,' she said. 'There is a purpose behind this, and we want to know what it is.'

'There are also time-tables and a packet of dollars.'

'They could be misleading. Concentrate on the scenes. The meaning is somewhere there.'

'Then start with; where is it?'

'I don't know,' she said.

'But you got there!' he said, incredulously.

'By private helicopter with the film crew, the actor and Garner with myself. All the trip Garner kept on about the script and we did all the work on it there so we saw nothing outside — or almost nothing. Certainly not enough to know where we were flying. Garner explained we had to do it in the plane because of the short time available at the house.'

'A script?'

'Don't be surprised. This is a professional sequence, everything planned and worked out beforehand. You can't go into a place and start shooting with the players doing anything they think of. Garner did the planning, with Andre, the photographer.'

'Where's he?'

'Anywhere. He, his girl and the model came over from Paris. They go all over the place, Andre and the girl. Garner had the address, not me.'

'So you don't know where the house is, nor the photographer.'

She gave a short shake of her head.

'So you went straight to this baronial hall, and what happened?'

'We went over the ground, from the terrace into the hall, the corridor and that library. All five of us together. There was a dress rehearsal, and then we began undress shots.'

'And then you just went through — this lot?'

'Oh no. There were hitches. There are always things that go wrong, shots that aren't right. Garner placed us, you see, and Andre arranged his stuff for that situation.'

'So Garner directed all this?'

'Yes.'

'Then it's got to be the house that matters.'

'Thank you. But yes, it must be.'

'But why the soft porn?'

'Andre would have sold short cut sequences for international magazines. That was the deal.'

'Oh, so there was a return?'

'There was always a return for Garner. You must have noticed that long before now.'

'I see. So it was rational and probably profitable. Andre would have taken some cost risk?'

'Of course. The French are sharp dealers.'

He went to the door and switched on more lights. It was dark outside then and he felt the desk lamp was tending to make things intimate.

She sat down in a chair beside the desk.

'I'll check the time tables tomorrow and see if I can find a similar print.'

'What about the ten thousand dollars?'

'I can't explain that, but I wouldn't try and spend any.'

He looked at her sitting back gracefully in the chair, and then, like flipping a negative, saw her naked in the chair. He looked away.

'You really think there's a lot in this, don't you?' he said, turning his head back towards her.

'Yes. He would never have gone to all this trouble for a thousand or two.'

'He could milk that out of the tills,' he said sourly.

She looked at him with sudden sharpness, and he felt his heart shrink a little. He had made an error. A stupid error, and she had caught it on the instant.

'Why do you say that?'

'Well, he could have done. We have a good turnover.'

'I see.'

He knew she saw too well. The uneasy feeling he had had, that she knew he had killed Garner became firmer, and he, watching her calm body, knew that her suspicion had been made certainty by his idiotic remark.

It was then that he first had the feeling that, to save himself, he would need to go to her. His fearful rage at the thought almost choked him. He closed his eyes, swallowed and strained to keep his arms steady and give no sign of the absurd emotion.

'What are you thinking?' she said.

He opened his eyes to slits and saw she was beginning to smile, just faintly, just enough to make him want to rush to her and smash his fist into her face and get rid of that smile forever.

He opened his eyes, the rage suddenly going like water down a sink, to leave the cold emptiness of fear.

'Nothing of use,' he said, in a dry

voice. 'The whole thing beats me.'

She watched him, then got up.

'I'm the thing that beats you,' she said. 'I can smell the sexual emotions a mile off.'

'I'd like to strangle you,' he said, with furious calm.

'Now I can hear it.' She passed him at a quiet, easy pace and went to the door. 'I am not in the mood for rape. Think of what we have discussed.'

She went. He heard her shut the front door. He smashed his fist into the back cushion of a chair, then suddenly felt close to tears of rage and a gathering cloud of helplessness.

Banquo, Banquo, walking through his head in glassy serenity and silent reproof — No, it wasn't Banquo. It was big, calm, fleshly Hagworth. Bloody whore. Bitch.

Then suddenly he turned, opened the door, ran through the hall, flung open the main door and then ran out along the short drive into the road.

She was sitting in her car. He thought she smiled a little when she saw him. He

81

ran to the car and leant in the window.

'Don't go — let's talk about it — more. Please — '

'Talk about what more?' she said quietly.

'This — whole business,' he said, desperate and not wanting to know why.

'What a little boy you are,' she said, with smiling gentleness. 'Get your head out!'

She drove off. The door pillar almost hit him as he drew back so that to avoid it he half turned, tripped and sat down on the pavement. He stayed there for some seconds, numbed with a fury his senses couldn't manage.

Then he felt the same queer cessation of feeling he had had when hitting Garner by the safe.

He got up, dusted his trousers with his hands, and went back indoors.

It began to come into his head that he would kill her as he had killed Garner, but with some kind of enjoyment.

He swept up the prints from the desk, stuffed them back in their envelopes and put everything back in the desk drawer.

He went into the kitchen. There was a note from Mrs Colman; 'Salad in frig, S.C.'.

He turned and went back into the hall. The tension and emotions of the past hours had left an acid vacuum in his stomach. He did not want to eat. He wanted to get out of the place, have a drink somewhere.

He drove to a pub on the other side of the town by the golf course. He had forgotten Partridge. When he got into the bar Partridge was there chatting up the barmaid. He would have left, but Partridge saw him.

The buyer stood drinks and made a few cracks about the customers, then brought something out of his coat pocket and laid it on the table.

It was a tiny leather golf bag with a set of miniature clubs sticking out of it.

'The legacy,' he said, with a sardonic grin.

'What?'

'Well, I thought it was odd when the will said golf clubs, because I don't think Garner ever played. He belonged to the club as a walking round member. That's all.'

Rayner shook the little clubs out of the bag on to the counter.

'Pretty,' he said.

'I think it must have been a prize for some competition or other, but how Garner got it I don't know.' Partridge sat back on his stool. 'How are you getting on with your pornographic heirloom?'

'I think he was cracked,' Rayner said shortly. 'Photos, scraps of old bus tables, menus, worn out socks and a key but no clue to where the lock is. What the hell did he ever keep such stuff for?'

'Did he do it as a joke on you? This was one on me, for sure.' He told a joke about a hoax. It was obscene, but somehow funny.

'He wouldn't have paid for a deposit box to put over a joke after he was dead.'

'That's the weird part, Jim. It all seems as if he knew his number was up.' He slipped in a short sharp joke about double numbers. 'Seriously, does it strike you?'

'How could he? Read it in his stars,

do you mean? He wasn't that sort.'

'Not really. No. I was thinking rather more along the lines that he fancied somebody had it in for him.'

'Who the hell would want to thump Garner?'

'He was a secretive sort of a bugger, you know. It always occurred to me he might have had other secrets than Hayworth, Janet, spinster. And he did own those flats. How the hell did he buy those on ten thousand a year plus bonuses? I mean, old lad, she moved in there about four years back and she wouldn't have done that if the flat hadn't been his. They are luxury flats. I should think sixty thousand quid's worth, and he never used them himself. Instead he hires a ropy old flat in the High Street. It just doesn't add up, unless he came into a lot of money all of a sudden.'

'Yes, I see what you mean, but he may have been saving all his life.'

'With that wife? I bet she boned his income.'

'Were they divorced?'

'I didn't hear the word ex-wife at all. Did you?'

'What about the wine stock he left you?'

'That was ill-starred,' said Partridge. 'When I enquired after it, I was told it wasn't there. On further enquiry I found that it had gone, illegally, down the steward's gullet. There will now be a committee meeting to consider the crime. Do you realise that sod left nothing but trouble for everyone he knew?'

'I'm beginning to think so.' Rayner signalled the barmaid to repeat the drink order.

Partridge told a quick joke about ex-wives.

'I wonder if the Hayworth will look round for another ageing but rich man? I mean, she won't get financial support from young ones, will she?'

'If you say those flats are worth sixty thousand she needn't be in a hurry to look. She's only thirty, you know.'

'Oh, you actually know that, do you?'

'I asked Pat to look it up once when everybody was arguing about her.'

'Well, there's an opening for you, lad.' Partridge laughed. 'Sixty thousand and tits galore, if you'll pardon the vulgarity.'

Rayner shrugged. 'You keep pushing her on to me. What's the matter? Are you tied up there somehow?'

'Oh no. I did try it on once. You know about spiders, do you? How he has to box around to get in the mating position with great skill, otherwise he gets killed. Well, I didn't box clever, and she hit me. She really hit me. I've never been able to hit a woman. It's a weakness. When she saw she'd hurt me she kept on hitting me. I fell down, then she kicked me. I was so full of hurt I was spitting. I don't know why I spat. I can't think of any reason. Luckily I hadn't got a tooth coming out. Well, when she'd really got me begging her to stop — you know what? She let me!'

He shook his head as if still bewildered. Rayner realised whisky was doing a lot of the talking, but it still wasn't the kind of thing bouncy Partridge would make-up against himself.

'It was a while back now. Two or three years, I suppose. I'm still mixed up in the head about it. I reckon she'd murder anybody for fourpence. And enjoy it,' he added sadly.

'Why didn't you run?'

'She had me up against a wall, old lad.'

'Is this why you keep egging me on?' Rayner signalled for more drinks. He had finished his.

'Oh, no, no, no,' said Partridge, shaking his head. 'She wouldn't hit you.'

'How do you know?'

'I don't *know*, but I have an instinct about behaviour in certain types of people. I must confess to you, people always did tend to hit me, and I often sense when they would like to. Also, I did crack too many jokes around her and she knew it.'

The new drinks came.

'My turn,' said Partridge, and paid. 'I had one hell of a time with the lady wife that night, and afterwards. You know, when she saw my face, Oh Heavens what's happened, call the police, get the ambulance, ring the fire engines — all the lot.'

'What did you say?'

'I said I walked into a fight outside a pub.'

'Good enough.' Rayner watched him. 'You're not getting around to saying Hayworth biffed Garner, are you?'

'There's no evidence anybody biffed him Jim lad. You know that — Oh, I see what you mean. Few coming into the flats and that. Motive. No. She's not the sort to bother with motives. She believes in the Divine Right of Queens . . . '

'Do you think she'll stay on now he's gone?'

'I can't guess,' Rayner said carelessly. 'She might go back to modelling.' Then through the alcoholic glow he realised he had slipped a bad one.

'Modelling? You don't mean for photographers? With a face like that? — ' He stopped and pointed. 'Not the face, then. Oho! Well, now — '

'Don't be a fool, Partridge.'

Partridge was blearily inspired.

'That porn he left you,' he said, jabbing at him with a finger. 'It wasn't her, was it? Is that how you know, Jim lad?'

'She mentioned it one day.' Rayner was angry. 'Trying to impress, I thought.'

'She doesn't try,' Partridge said slowly. 'She *is*.'

'I can't follow this Scotch grammar.'

Rayner was angry and frightened. It seemed he kept letting things go which he should have kept tightly in his head. He must, subconsciously, have been taking too much for granted that the accident verdict would finish the matter.

'You've got the wrong end of the stick,' Rayner said. 'Don't start shouting that about. She modelled fashions. That sort of thing. Far as I can remember. I wondered why she wasn't a buyer for women's stuff.'

'Oh, that's spoilt it,' Partridge said, and drank. 'We already have darling Mitzi, beautiful outside buyer and connoozer of girds for lovely loins. There's a woman for you! Straight as a bargepole, mark you, but such grace! Such style!'

He spread out his hands descriptively,

went backwards on the stool, which tottered into a man behind him.

'Sorry, sorry!' Partridge cried as the man helped him back to the upright position.

Rayner got up.

'See you,' he said, and left.

Outside the night was cool. He stood in the park by his car trying to clear his head from fear, whisky and the pressure of trying to decide what he should do.

When he let things go — things that didn't matter all that much in themselves — they could easily gather up the passions of other people, and from that, to yet others, so that in the end, a number of people would start to look for who had started the rumour.

He had started it, but most of all he feared the anger of Janet Hayworth when she realised that Partridge knew.

He got into the car, and for the third time drove back to the flats. Lights were on when he mounted the steps and for the third time that night, rang the bell.

5

Again there was no response to the ring. Again he began to feel anger rising, and at the second ring his exasperation became almost fury.

The door opened when, for the sake of luxuriating in rage, he almost hoped it wouldn't.

She stood there in a kaftan, the light behind her shining on her glasses, making her eyes invisible.

'Well?' she said, without surprise or much interest.

'I want a word,' he said.

'Say it. You haven't someone with you, have you?'

'No.'

'Well? There is no one to hear. Go on.'

He stood there, straining against anger and an impulse to hit her and destroy that maddening calm.

'What's the matter with you? Say it!'

'I bumped into Partridge.'

'So?'

'He knows about your photographic work — the early work.'

'You told him.'

'I did not!'

'Then how did it come up?'

'He was trying to be funny about what you did before you came to the office.'

'He wasn't interested. Partridge is only interested in himself. Secretly a masochist. Did you know that?'

'Partridge?' he said, surprised above his anger.

'He likes to be beaten. He is twisted. What did you say to start him on my career?'

'He was talking about these flats. Wondering if you were going to retire. He was rambling on.'

'You're cut. I suppose he was?'

He paused a moment to save himself from shouting.

'I am not. He was. It's his hobby.'

She turned and walked away, leaving the door open. He stood a moment, then went in after her. She stopped in the middle of a large, split-level living room and turned as he came up. She hit him hard across the face with her hand.

'You told him,' she said, as he staggered back in surprise and hurt. 'You let it out. Then he guessed about the photographs in the packets. So now he'll be looking. You are an irresponsible bloody fool. You haven't thought one sensible thing about this inheritance, nor have you done anything to find out what it means.'

He stood there, rigid, staring at her.

'The only way we can find the meaning is to do it together,' she said. 'I knew Garner, but I don't know enough about you to begin the link-up between what he meant and what you are.'

'What I am?' His face stung, but somehow it exhilarated him and made the puzzle suddenly presented the most important thing at that moment.

'Yes. He knew something which I don't. Something about you. I know that this whole thing was cooked up by him, and I think it was left in that way in case something happened to him before he could do it himself.'

If he asked a question about what she said it might reveal to her that he knew Garner had been a crook. To let that out would be dangerous. He began to lose his passion in the colder mind of wariness.

'You mean it was something he meant to do with you, and if he died before it was done, I should take his place? At what?'

'Hidden treasure, perhaps,' she said, and sat on the arm of an overstuffed chair. 'He was fascinated by finding fortune somehow, somewhere.'

'Every gambler suffers from that. Was he a gambler?'

'In a way.' She looked at him steadily through her big glasses. 'I have the idea that you did not find him in the office because you saw a light on that night.'

'When he died, you mean? Why? What's funny about it?'

'Nothing funny — so far as I know. I just have this quaint idea that you had arranged to see him in the office that night.'

He kept firm control, so firm that he began to feel confident that he could handle what he felt was coming.

'You mean that *he* arranged to see *me*. He was boss.'

'But this wasn't directly to do with business.'

'Something private between us? But there was nothing.'

'I feel that you had some idea he was fiddling the accounts, you know.' She spoke softly in a silky voice.

'That would be difficult for him, wouldn't it?'

'He was in sole charge of the branch. His figures went forward.'

He moved round a chair and sat down, facing her.

'But you always vetted the figures,' he said.

'The figures he gave me,' she said, and smiled. 'You know, I felt that you went to the office that night to see what he really was doing, and that he knew one day you would do that.'

He moved in the seat, watching her.

'You credit him with supernatural

powers,' he said. His firm, quick awareness began to shiver a little at a new background idea that it might not be Banquo haunting him, but that something of Garner was still alive in him somewhere.

'He was unusually gifted in interpreting the moves that people never made. He seemed able to see through them at the very times they were trying to be opaque. It was an unnerving gift.'

It was not unnerving enough, he thought, or Garner would have been alive now.

'Let us go back,' she went on. 'I think you suspected he was milking the takings and called in specially to find him at it.'

'I didn't. But what difference would it have made? I found him dead.'

'And you rang the police,' she said, 'which shows great presence of mind.' She smiled again.

He sat back.

'I don't see how this has to do with the legacy.'

'I am suggesting he knew something

about you, and that he was sure you'd look in at the office one night to see what he was doing, because he knew you suspected.'

Rayner began to feel uneasy again, but firmness reasserted itself as he spoke.

'Well, if that was what he was supposed to be doing, why wasn't there something funny about the money that night? Or do you suggest I pinched the cash he had meant to pilfer?'

'Not at all,' she said. 'He had a shrewd intelligence, like a fox. Once he thought someone suspected, he would cease to use that method. He was, in his personal way, a very methodical person.'

An idea shot into his head, like a falling star through a night sky, leaving but a fading fiery trail in the back of his brain.

Had she been in the office that night?

The quiet chill of that icy sky disappeared. If she had been there, all this would never have happened and the days following the murder would have been spent in the arms of the law.

'So he was methodical,' he said. 'How

does that affect the purpose of the legacy?'

'Let's begin with Garner. Assume he was fiddling money from the company, and that he was at heart an unfulfilled crook.'

'If he got all this out of fiddling the books he was a crook,' Rayner said, looking round.

'Further, assuming he had an idea for one big final robbery which would set him up for life, but which he thought was so clever he left it to somebody else if he died, so that the robbery would still be done as a sort of epitaph. He was a sentimental man, about himself.'

'Yes. We've been on these lines before, I think. You mean that the reason for the pictures is the house. Find the house and you find where the fortune is. Very true. But you don't find out what it is, nor how it's hidden.'

'No. And nor do you find how Garner found out about it, because it wouldn't be a public property which he had marked. It wouldn't be something difficult to sell. Most likely it would be money. That was his ideal profit medium.'

'Well, where did you fly from that day?'

'From Denton's Farm at Orton Cross. It has a private pad there that is used by business firms.'

'And how long did you fly?'

'An hour — just over. It seems to give a radius of about a hundred and twenty miles.'

'Which is a lot of land, and bound to be some sea. But the direction. Did you notice the sun?'

'Garner kept us busy, and I think I mentioned the plane seemed to circle quite a lot — or it felt like it. No. I've tried, you know. Garner made sure we wouldn't know then.'

'Perhaps the bus timetables are the key. Find a comparable one with the destinations on and it might give a pointer. But the dollars — ?'

'And the socks and the key to the razors.'

'It's a fine key. It must fit a good case.' He stared at her. 'And more likely, it's one bloody great hoax.' He got up.

100

'Don't go just yet,' she said, calmly. 'You forget; you let Partridge know about the photographs.'

'I did not. But still — What?'

'He will assume that's what the legacy was; pictures of me.'

'Let him.'

'He'll ferret. That's what he does.'

'Again — let him. And further about this. What gave Garner the idea of this nude bawdy performance? Why? Why did the photographer come over and all the rest of it? Was the pay good?'

'I will expand on what I told you earlier. When I began that career they stuck other heads on, and that was popular. This was all for sales on the Continent, you understand. Then somebody had the idea of wearing a hat with a veil, and that was very successful. After all, it was the body that was wanted and the veil idea seemed to add something for the gawpers. In that way I became quite famous and made money.'

'Then Garner turned up, and we formed a partnership. There was some evil in both of us that appealed, but little else. Also, I was then twenty-four and tired of travelling about and posing for hours. I really was sick of it.'

'Garner seemed to have plenty of money. At first I thought he owned the firm. Anyhow, during the time I spent as his secretary I had offers now and again from photographers who thought of a comeback, but did nothing about it. It was Garner who realised that if he set up such a session, it would, because of my deplorable fame, probably cost him nothing.'

'You are very open about all this,' Rayner said, surprised.

'Because I know you can't get away,' she said.

He felt as if he had been pierced with a shaft of ice through his stomach and caught his breath for a moment. He shrugged, and warmth came back slowly, flowing right through him, making his legs weak.

That sudden flood of fear left a smaller wave following it; fear that once again his inbuilt weakness in too strong reaction was getting worse.

For the first time the idea came to him that he was basically mentally unstable, liable to violent changes that could destroy him if he did not face the reality.

* * *

'These moments of silence puzzle me,' she said, watching him. 'As if something is arresting inside you. Have you some kind of tummy?'

'Occasionally,' he said. 'I haven't eaten yet.'

'I'll get something,' she said. 'No one can plot on an empty stomach.' She got up, gave a short gesture for him to follow her and walked through an opening into a kitchen diner with openwork shelves, and tendrils of yellowing weeds clawing with their last strength at the upright poles of the structure.

She put bread in the toaster and broke eggs into a pan.

'Try altering the sequence of the pictures,' she said. 'The way we took them didn't follow straight on because of lighting and other problems.'

'Looking for what in the prints themselves?'

'Something that might cover a safe — No, that's too simple. Too straightforward. With his little hobby a clue had to mean something that meant something else which would give you the clue to the real thing.'

'But this series was a production which he had planned beforehand. It could not be that involved. But there are certain ideas which begin to suggest themselves.'

'Such as?'

'That the bus tables indicate the place and the times when a raid would be possible.'

'You sound quite professional.' She laughed ironically.

'What else would you call it? The other thing is that the serial numbers on some of the dollar bills give the code to a combination lock. I've seen both ideas in crime films or books somewhere.'

She gave him eggs on toast and poured red wine from an opened bottle into two glasses. She took her glass and leant against the open shelves.

'We saw no one at all that day at that house,' she said, staring across the room. 'No servants, no gardeners, no host, guest, dog, cat — nothing of a household.'

'But didn't any of you ask questions? Something must have been said about a place like that?'

'Garner sliced them all away, and remember, three of the four were French and did most of their talking to each other. They were also dedicated professionals. A beautiful house is a backdrop to them.'

'But you asked Garner?'

'He started to make teasing jokes about not telling me. I kicked him out of here and he stayed out for three months, pleading and wheedling and whispering through the keyhole. He was pathetic when he wasn't a villain. To a woman, if you understand me.'

'But still he didn't tell you?'

'I didn't bring it up again.'

★ ★ ★

Next day Janet Hayworth did not arrive at the office until ten. Rayner noticed it specially, because her absence worried him oddly. As if she had run away. He would not trust her if she ran away. Not that he trusted her as it was, but common greed bound them together for the time being. If success came, that would be the time of splitting up, in one way or another.

Last night he had wondered just what way that would be.

When she came at ten, he waited a few minutes and then went into her office with a handful of papers. She wasn't there, but in Mann's office. She had a satchel type handbag lying on the end of her desk. He wondered whether to open it, but decided she was too near for him to take such a risk.

It was eleven before she came into his office, when he was free from a visit from a paint firm traveller.

'I think I have the tables,' she said. 'But it's a new edition. Long distance buses. Leeds.'

'Leeds?' he said. 'You wouldn't have

106

got there in the time in the aircraft you described.'

'They are long distance buses. I should have to compare with the cut pages.'

'I'll take you back at lunch time.'

'I'll begin walking. Pick me up. We don't want the office to notice anything new.'

He picked her up beyond the Town Hall at one-five, Mrs Colman was somewhat aggressive at being disturbed in the middle of her cleaning. He explained they had come for some papers, and she was momentarily stilled with astonishment at his pleasant manner, though not guessing what such guile cost him.

They went into the study and compared the cut tables with the new one. They agreed, though here and there were detail changes.

'The cut pages are out of order,' she said. 'Did you do that?'

'No. I have put everything back as it came out. Now look. On the full copy there are initial letters at the top of each page. Take those in the same order as the cut sheets and see if it spells anything.'

'Well, we must start somewhere,' she said, and brought a ballpoint and notepad from her bag. 'You read.'

'It'll take a minute or two to make sure which page it is.'

He began to compare the pages again, carefully keeping the order of the cut pages as he put them down. When he had done eight she dropped the pen on the desk top.

'That's it. Mallingford.'

'But that's only thirty miles.'

'I said the pilot circled a lot. That's it, for sure. Lord Malling's country seat. He lives in Jersey because of the taxes, but flies back whenever tax allows and scoots again before time is up. That's it.'

Rayner sat back in the desk chair.

'What on earth can be hidden there? I'm not game for stealing Rembrandts or Botticellis. I wouldn't touch that with a bargepole.'

'Oh, you would touch something, then?' she said, in that soft, silky voice.

He realised then that for the first time

he had admitted his criminal intentions over the whole business. Before then it had been a business of trying to decipher a crazy man's dying joke, but until she made that remark he had not realised the openness of his criminal intent.

'I have been thinking of some kind of potty hidden treasure,' he said. 'I am not starting a career as a burglar.'

'But you will,' she said gently, and looked at her watch. 'Let us go. We can take a snack on the way back to the office.'

'Just before we go,' he said, 'why do you suspect me of having done something evil?'

'Do I?' She looked at him and smiled. 'You invent my meaning to any question before I have given the answer. I can see you anticipating it.'

'It's just that I believe all men are guilty.'

'But not of crime. As far as this business goes, I had a legacy which made me wonder what it was supposed to be about. I may be wrong in thinking that it's about anything, but you believe there is something in it. You believe so strongly that you push me into trying to prove you are right.'

'I want to know. Curiosity is my Big Thing. I can't help it. Further, it brings me amusement. In this case, I was involved in the puzzle long before it reached you.'

'Oh yes. I'm not trying to deprive you in any part of whatever it turns out to be. If it's of any value, then it may be worth our time. Further, it's a challenge. But it is not criminal. I have done nothing, and, unless there's a promise of a lot of money, I'm not going to step anywhere over the boundaries of the law. I hope you understand.'

'I understand you have made an opening speech for the Defence. Forget it. We are solving a puzzle. We know the house now. What we have to find is what the something is and where in the house it is.'

He nodded. They went.

* * *

He returned at six-fifteen. Mrs Colman came into the hall to meet him as soon as he came.

'A lady's called,' she said. 'I've put her in the lounge. A Mrs Garnish, I think she said.' She went back into the kitchen.

Rayner felt uneasy. He looked into the hall mirror, straightened his tie, then went into the lounge, a big room with french windows on to the garden, where, in summer, his father would sometimes absent-mindedly push in his wheelbarrow from gardening and fall asleep in a large armchair.

Mrs Garner was sitting in that chair. She got up at once.

'Mr Rayner, I hope you don't mind me coming. It's about the will. I'm wondering whether to see a solicitor, but it may be all just one of his bad jokes. Do you mind telling me what he really left for you?'

She looked almost wistful, he thought.

'Not at all,' he said. 'There were some dirty pictures, a couple of old time tables, the pair of socks and the key to the razors, but it doesn't say where in the world they are, so why he took the trouble, I can't think.'

'Then it was just a silly joke?'

'I think they all were. Partridge, our buyer, was left golf clubs, but he found they were little toy ones, and the wine he was supposed to have had all been drunk years ago.'

'Oh, I see,' she said slowly. 'But what about the flats?'

'Ah, yes. I expect there is a catch in that, too. He probably sold it and paid off the mortgage with the money, so there is nothing left.'

'But you don't know?'

'Oh, no. It's none of my business. I don't want to be involved.' He looked at her again. 'Do you know, I wouldn't be surprised if you didn't get most of what there was. I don't really see how he could have had much money to leave.'

She looked sulky.

'Well, I certainly never saw any money when we were together. He was forever grumbling about bills and making me try to cut down. He was a mean man. I thought he would have saved, but he had this woman — '

'In the office it was thought that she shared all expenses, paid him rent and so on,' he said, and felt surprised at standing up for Hagworth until he realised he was merely fencing Mrs Garner off making trouble.

'Do you really think those flats belong to somebody else?' she said.

For the first time he realised that she was a bigger idiot than she had appeared at the funeral. All her spite had gone away and left a woman rather pathetically in need of help.

He felt better, pleased by his rising confidence.

'Of course, if they do belong elsewhere, it would make no difference to Miss Hayworth. She is a sitting tenant, and so long as she pays her rent, there is very little anyone can do about her.'

'No. I see. Well — ' She seemed about to leave but then stopped and looked at him with her head cocked to one side. 'The socks. They became a bone of contention between us. He insisted, and I refused. I bought him other socks with nylon heels but he wanted those old socks. It was just something to get at me.

'He even started inventing things about them and made threats. He once said my fortune would run out of the holes in the heels, just to make out I was a slut who would do nothing to save myself. It wasn't fair.'

He thought she was going to cry, but she straightened up and left. When he closed the front door after her he went back into the study and for the first time, looked closely at the socks.

Outside she hurried along the pavement, turned the corner and got into a waiting car where a woman was sitting at the wheel.

'He said it was a lot of rubbish,' she said, as her companion drove off. 'But I think he's a liar. He made excuses for everything and said the flats were sold before he died.'

'Lying little bastard,' said the driver.

6

Janet Hayworth was not so sure at first that she had heard her bell ring, the peal was so short, almost diffident, she thought. She was not expecting anyone, but in the present state of affairs Rayner might call at any time. Only the brief small ring did not sound to her like his angry push at the bell.

She was surprised to see the woman there.

'Oh, Mrs Garner,' she said, with the practised charm of a devious secretary, 'do come in.' She smiled.

Mrs Garner smiled uncertainly. She looked so shy as to be almost mouselike. Janet Hayworth did not trust mouselike looks and probed right through the appearance.

The widow sat down and accepted a small sherry after Janet had taken her into the split-level lounge.

'I'm sorry to have called out of the blue

like this — ' she said, still uncertain.

'Really, it doesn't matter at all. I am not going out this evening. Something is worrying you, Mrs Garner?'

She came right to the point and Mrs Garner seemed taken aback for a moment.

'Well, as you can imagine, I've been very upset about all this business. His insults — Can you understand?'

'Of course,'said Janet, warmly.

'It's silly, really. We've been apart several years now. We should have divorced a long time back.'

'Why didn't you?'

'He wouldn't agree,' she said, suddenly sharp.

'He wouldn't?'

'No. There was no reason why he should have refused, except spite, I suppose. He never forgave me for leaving. Not because he loved me, but because he was afraid it made him look a fool. He never liked to look foolish about women.'

'I don't suppose men do, in general. They are afraid it makes them seem lacking in sexual pull. They like you to think they have a lot of that.'

Janet smiled. Mrs Garner's eyes shone a little with some inner surprise she did not show on her features.

'He told me that *you* wouldn't agree to divorce,' added Janet.

'I'm not surprised at that. He always liked to blame somebody else for his weaknesses. But then, of course, you knew him well enough not to need me to talk about his little traits.'

'Well, he had quite a few, Mrs Garner.' She sat down with elegance. 'How can I help you?'

'It was — about these flats,' Mrs Garner said in rather a rush. 'I have a close friend who keeps pushing me to do something, although I don't know what there is to do, quite honestly.'

'He left me his interest in the flats,' Janet said. 'And that amounted to five hundred pounds.'

'What!'

'Mrs Garner, I had a career before I came here in which I made a comfortable sum of money. This was invested by a skilful solicitor, and when these flats came on the market, I hadn't enough. I borrowed the balance from Mr Garner, and repaid him with interest in the form of rent. Only five hundred pounds remained unpaid when he died.'

'Only five hundred — ' The widow was stunned with incredulity, but recovered. 'Is that all? I thought it was worth thousands — '

'It is, but they're mine.'

'Yes, I see — I didn't understand — Not at all. No. But I thought they were in his name — '

'They were until the debt was settled. Of course,' Janet added, 'if you made a claim, my Bank would gladly pay you five hundred pounds, but only if you proved at law that the money is rightfully yours. That is, if you contest the will. But to do that and succeed would get you the five hundred and cost you five thousand in lawyers' fees. You know lawyers. I'm afraid that is the ugly face of reality.'

'Yes, I understand that.' The widow looked into her glass and seemed sad. 'Of course, I never really knew anything

of what he was doing after we parted
— that is, in the business way.' She
looked up. 'But how on earth did he
get all that money to lend you? He never
had any when we were together.'

'But was he open about his business
affairs?'

'I suppose whatever he did tell me was
lies. He used to lie about anything, even
to justify a tantrum or a mistake. He
must have been very different in business,
or they would never have kept him on.'

'He was a shrewd man,' Janet said.
'And his strange sort of humour rather
tickled people. Men, anyway.' She looked
up with new interest. 'Do you work?'

'I have a position in a library. It's
interesting, but only because of the books,
I'm afraid. I don't get on much with
people any more. They are too stupid.'

She raised her head sharply and looked
away, then a new thought softened her
anger.

'Did he have any business interest
outside the firm, do you know?'

'I couldn't say. As you just pointed
out, he didn't give away much about

his interests. But the will didn't indicate that he had.'

'No — only the flats,' said the widow, 'and they really weren't his. But, I mean, he had a good salary and you paid him rent; he must have spent a lot.'

'Well, I imagine my rent paid his, and I don't really know what pay he did get.'

The widow shifted uneasily in her chair.

'There is something that worries me, but I'm not sure I really ought to say such a thing. I — ' She faded out at the start of a sentence.

'What is it?'

'Do you think he could have been murdered?'

'Well, naturally,' said Janet, quietly, 'that's a point that everybody must have considered, but if he was — why? It seems no cash was missing that night, and the safe was open.'

'Yes, of course. It's somehow just not possible to believe he killed himself like that. He was always so very careful.'

'Anyone can slip up.'

'Yes, of course. Except I just can't

imagine him letting anything pass by him.' She smiled at last. 'I suppose these things always give one a jolt. But still, it's very nice of you to have seen me.'

When Janet had closed the door behind her, she stood at the window and watched her walk down the drive.

'A deceitful little bitch,' she murmured. 'I would sooner confide in a parliamentary candidate.'

★ ★ ★

The widow walked along the road to the waiting car.

'A hard bitch,' she said as she got in. 'But she knows what she's doing.'

'Do you think she killed him?' the driver said.

'What for? He only owned five hundred pounds worth of the property. The rest was hers before.'

'Did you believe that?'

'She isn't the sort to say something that she can't prove when it comes to that sort of thing. We shall have to find something else.'

'And did she pay him rent, do you think?'

'I'm sure she did. I don't feel she'd have played a kept woman. More likely she kept him for amusement, or for some business reason. I wonder why she worked as a secretary when she had money enough to put into that place. She said she had a career before.'

'What as — a prostitute?'

'Well, we could find out, but I don't quite see how it would help. She borrowed some money from Arthur, and the five hundred is all that remains. The will, now I remember, was so worded that I realise now it was a bit of a joke, leaving her something which was, practically, already hers. Now I think of it, it was like the rest of the bequests; a twisted joke.'

'You swallowed her story,then?'

'What I swallowed was that she could prove it. That's what matters.'

★ ★ ★

Janet Hayworth answered her phone on the kitchen extension.

'It's Rayner. I thought I'd tell you Dame Garner was here earlier. I think she was after something, but I'm not sure. Then it occurred to me she might call on you — '

'She has called. Just gone. She was on a dig. All she got were facts. But she didn't apologise for calling me a whore in front of the mourners.'

'I think she hardly noticed what she said. My impression was she really expected something useful out of that will. Did she know about you before he died?'

'I should think so. What line did she take with you?'

'Oh, shy widow. But a shy widow after what I really had in that deposit box, and I told her it was what the will said; a collection of rubbish. She said something about the socks.'

'Oh?'

'I've looked at them since. They were mended once but not the last time. Do you know about knitting or darning patterns? I don't.'

'Are there holes still?'

'Yes. It seems he made some remark about her fortune running out through the holes. One of his joke puzzles, perhaps.'

Janet paused.

'I'm coming over. I saw a small microscope in that study.'

'Yes. Father uses one for studying bugs. Yes. All right. Come over. Something might connect up with what she said.'

As Rayner put the phone down he realised not only that she was telling him what she would do, but also that he was beginning to rely on her help in solving the mad conundrum.

And in his mind already the vision of treasure had formed. Garner had had something hidden somewhere, he was sure. The systematic fiddling of the takings over several years had gained him some substantial profit and he was hardly likely to have advertised his gains by buying a block of two luxury flats. Some investment from his normal life, yes, but not anything that would make people sit up and say, 'How on earth did he get that?' No good crook advertises his profits by spending too soon.

Janet arrived within minutes of the call. They went into the study.

'Tell me just what she said, then I'll report my bit,' she said, looking round at a microscope on a corner table.

The recounting was done quickly and, by Janet, expertly, as if she had taken shorthand notes.

'What's she after?' Rayner said. 'Does she really think there's something she doesn't know about? If she — Damn.' He turned as the phone began to ring. 'Yes? Freda! God, I'm sorry! Garner's left such a terrible mess — loose ends all over — people keep getting on to me — Yes. Right away. Of course.' He put the phone down. 'Bloody woman. I'd forgotten her. Blast it.'

'Stood her up?' Janet said.

'Yes. I'll have to go. It could be a nuisance — not to us but to me. I don't want any nuisances now.'

She watched him a moment. He was rattled. He seemed to be easily rattled, she thought. As if everybody knew he had murdered Garner . . .

He cursed as he got into his car. To

forget her what seemed like a second time could blow things up. To forget things in any case could blow things up. Why had he begun forgetting? Why, at a time like this, when Garner was still in the public mind?

Hagworth was watching all the time, but she wouldn't cross him. They were depending on each other. They shared the secret of Garner's fortune, or at least, of finding it. He had meant them to find it, though why could only have been another twisted part of his fantasy of puzzles.

Garner had been twisted all through. He had twisted himself into his own death. And perhaps even that had amused him.

As he drove a slow freeze crawled through Rayner's veins when the thought came that Garner had known he would die. He had known he would be murdered. Perhaps he had known who would murder him.

He drove fast to meet Freda and kept trying excuses over and over in his mind. Best to stick to the business of left-overs from Garner. That would be beyond his control. He envisaged a horde of bewildered business firms ringing him for guidance on this, that and the other which Garner had failed to pass on to his successor.

Of course, Garner hadn't thought of needing a successor. Then how had he expected to die? Why, only a few weeks before his death, had he prepared that deposit box with the stuff inside it?

What had given him the idea that he might die? And why had he picked Rayner to solve the puzzle?

He got to the car park where he had arranged to meet Freda and drove in. There were only a few cars parked. Two or three were like Freda's, but they were empty. He stopped in a central space and got out. He could see no one sitting in any car, though he walked up to three different cars with headrests that looked like people.

She was not there. She hadn't waited.

He stood by his car watching the lights come on along the streets.

She hadn't waited. Of course she hadn't

waited. It was normal to be angry and drive away when a lover didn't turn up. He would have to do something, take flowers or some gift to make his peace — but he would have to know when Freddy wouldn't be there, and Freddy was a pretty free agent at his office. He came and went as he pleased, as outside engagements called, and called home when his way lay near his house.

It would be difficult to make sure when he wouldn't be there, and he didn't think Freda would answer him on the phone. She had made her comment by refusing to wait longer. She would make it awkward for him. That was certain. Why the hell he had taken her that night he couldn't think. Looking back it seemed like some idiotic means of getting out of the weakening embrace of his troubles. And it had doubled them up. He didn't want more enemies now.

As he got into the car her absence made it seem as if the shadowy figures of the local world were gathering against him. It was Depression. He must not have Depression.

As he started he tried to think how this feeling of dread had started and then realised it had begun when he had seen Janet Hayworth watching him across that damned open grave.

He drove away, then switched from going to his home to the big pub where he had met Freddy that night. He might go back with Freddy and snatch the chance of making up, smoothing over, putting things straight.

He went in. The place was busy but he could not see Freddy. He ordered a large Scotch and took it to a table away from the bar.

Curiously, Freda had come right into the front of his mind; the rest of the turmoil of new events in his life receded. So wrapt in his thoughts and struggles for an easy solution, he did not see Freddy come in and fade into the chattering crowd which cut off his sight of the bar itself. He was startled when Freddy appeared and sat at the table facing him, holding his drink in his hand. He stared at Rayner in an odd, fixed kind of way.

'Freda's blown her bloody top,' he

said, still staring. 'I came out to get away from it. She blows, now and again. She said she'd gone to her Mother's but came roaring back, bursting with tears of rage — '

'What was the matter?' Rayner said, trying not to look as taut as he felt.

'She said you tried to rape her the other night,' Freddie said, in an odd, passionless way. 'You weren't that pissed, were you?'

Rayner could not speak for several seconds. He had known Freda was hard, but he hadn't thought she would let rage go as far as telling Freddy such a thing.

'I can't believe it,' he said, huskily.

'Well, you know, women do have this sort of fantasy,' Freddie said, looking away at last. 'Their magazines are full of it. But I didn't think Freda would drift off like that.'

'I just don't understand,' Rayner said, his voice rattling in a dry throat.

'She didn't, sort of, make a pass at you and you turned her down? That would make her bloody mad, but rape — ! In a chap's own house — No.' He looked back at Rayner.

'But why? I don't understand.'

'She's been bottling it up, it seems. Then I suppose something upset her and she just blew it.' He looked away again. 'Actually, I don't mind telling you there's been trouble before about this sort of thing. A feller called Jameson. What happened there I don't know, but he pushed off out of the picture and it blew over. The trouble is she has such a foul temper and she'll lie her head off. Just wants to screw me up.'

Freddy seemed to be getting confused and saying things he did not mean to say in the process of putting forward some case of his own, but was not sure that his case or the listener was right.

He was very angry. Rayner could see that, but did not seem to know where to shoot.

'But why did she say it?' Rayner said.

Freddy leant on the table.

'Well, look. She was in a bad rage, and she let it out to sort of hit me because she felt so wild. To sort of accuse me of not caring one way or the other. Unfortunately, it's got a bit like that between us. I don't mind telling you that.' He looked around, smiled and signalled to someone he knew, then turned back to Rayner. 'Well, she elaborated. She said you tried and then she agreed for fear of getting me down and starting a fight or something. I don't believe that. She's the rowing sort.' He sat back, and shrugged. 'Well, that's what she said.'

'I don't know what to say.'

'I'll put my cards on the table, Rayner. I believe none of this rape, but I'm quite ready to believe you two had it off. It wouldn't be new to me. She's involved my friends before. But not again, Rayner. I'm going to the Court this time. You can have her. I'll be a fool no longer.'

He got up and left, leaving his drink unfinished on the table.

Rayner sat back in his seat and shut his eyes.

Why in hell had he touched the bloody woman? Why?

He opened his eyes and took a drink, trying to appear calm, as if he fancied everyone in the big room was looking at him.

Anger returned after a short interval of confusion. In anger he realised that he had not hurt Freddy. He had done Freddy a good turn. If Freddy hadn't found him waiting to find Freddy, Freddy would have gone on looking till he found him somewhere else. Freddy wanted to be rid of her.

Remembering the scene of that night, with Freddy trying to obey her, to hide things from her wrath, to please her and stop her hurting him, he wondered how he had not spotted the situation then.

Had Freddy been as drunk as he'd seemed, or had he known what was likely to happen, and just waited? Had Freddy seen through the Call to Mother's and just waited for her to come back and begin the confrontation?

What the hell had happened to his head that he had forgotten the appointment with her? No wonder she'd screamed the house down. She had been the woman scorned and proved Congreve right. Hell hath no fury, and he'd got the Hell.

Suddenly, his mind changed. Why bother? If Freddy divorced her, what did it matter? Let her go. If she tried to hang on to him he could kick her off. He owed her nothing.

He began to feel as he had the night he had killed Garner, firm, cold, sure of himself. He had hated Garner, and now he hated Freda. There were solutions to everything. He had solved Garner. He would solve the Freda problem as it seemed fit, though he fancied that after the blow-up at home, she wouldn't demean herself to come dragging after him.

He finished his drink and left the inn.

Janet Hayworth was still at his house when he got there. She had the prints spread out on the desk again and he saw the socks lying by the phone at the end of the display.

She looked up.

'What's happened?' she said sharply. 'You look sick!'

He was momentarily frozen by the realisation that his mental state showed so clearly on his face. But it was no use trying to pretend nothing had happened when she could see the truth so clearly.

'That bloody woman,' he said. 'She went home and told her bloody husband I raped her!'

'Which woman?' she said.

'Freda Jarvis,' he said, after a slight hesitation.

'And did you?'

'No.'

'You mean she agreed,' Janet said, looking down at the desk. 'Is there going to be publicity?'

'I don't know. He wants a divorce.'

'Whatever Jarvis wants he'll get. He's got money and lawyers in his pocket. But it'll take time to come out. The main trouble is that she might start hanging round, asking what you propose to do. We don't want that.'

She watched him. Once again he felt the uneasiness that had floated on the air across the open grave. She *knew*, this woman. She *knew*. Like a witch. She could read people.

She gave a faint smile, shrugged and

nodded to the desk top.

'The socks,' she said, 'have been glued.'

'Glued?' he said. 'What to try and mend them?'

'No. To make the frayed wool ends stiff and form spikes.'

He went closer to the desk.

'What for?'

'There are, altogether, twenty-six pictures in the sequence, and there are twenty-six letters in the alphabet. Now one thing I did know about Garner was his childish method of making puzzles. Mixed-up letters forming words would have appealed to his sense of cleverness. What we have to do is think of a word which would have appealed to that twisted sense of his and we get a sequence of the pictures.'

'What word, and how many letters?' he said.

7

'I don't know what word, or how many letters,' Janet Hayworth said, 'but it can't have the same letter twice.'

Rayner walked to the fireplace and came back again, restless, somehow apprehensive and trying to think himself out of tension.

'A favourite word?' he said. 'A pet of his.'

'All the curses I remember have double letters somewhere, and the only one that hasn't he didn't like. No, I think it's a name.'

'Janet,' he suggested.

'It doesn't seem long enough,' she said, 'but we'll try.'

She picked out the prints in accordance with the numbers of the letters. They both looked.

'There is a sequence,' he said.

She nodded. 'Yes, but it doesn't go far

enough. It looks more like the steps of a dance now.'

He turned away, impatient, irritated.

'Why was he so twisted? What kind of bloody joke was this for him? He had to be dead before he could see if it worked!'

She looked calmly at him as he started to pace again. She watched for a second or two, then picked up one of the socks. The heel holes were such that laid flat, the top one allowed a complete view through the bottom one.

'He made one of these deliberately,' she said. 'How can you wear a hole through the instep side?'

She placed the sock over the second print. The hole framed one side of the fanlight over the great main door. She went back to the first and did the same. It picked out part of the wall beside the front door, inside the hall.

'The burglar alarm,' she said. 'Now we're under way. The burglar alarm. The fanlight from outside.' She moved the sock. 'The corridor wall going in towards the big room . . . Now back to the panelled side of the stairs, framing one particular panel . . . The last one inside the room and framing the panelled wall . . . '

'A safe behind the panel,' he said, bending over. 'Assume that. Now we've got the burglar alarm beside the door, and the fanlight. By the look of it one could reach the alarm by reaching down through the fanlight. Okay. What's behind the stairs' panel?'

'Main control for another alarm?' she suggested. 'Or the main fuses to cut everything out?'

'What about the corridor?'

'It marks one panel there. Might be some other alarms there — guarding the panel in the big room, perhaps.'

He began to pace again.

'If you are right, how the hell did he get to know all this?'

She sat down in the desk chair.

'We know the owner is away half the year because of tax. Supposing the place is let out on short periods, to cover expenses — ?'

He stopped and turned.

'Garner rented it? That would answer the question of how he got to know — But if he had the opportunity, why didn't he nick the stuff then?'

'He would have been caught at once.' She smiled.

He stopped walking.

'Yes, but all temporary tenants would have been suspected even if he burgled some time after. So it's more likely whatever he wanted wasn't there then but he knew it would be at some later date.'

'That would be a solution.'

'That's only five prints,' he said. 'What message is in the other twenty-one? Let's just do the sock spotting on each one. Now we know how it works, it should be easier to find the word backwards.'

A bell sounded. Rayner turned angrily towards the door.

'Someone called?' she said, and looked at her watch. 'Perhaps it's your woman — to beg forgiveness.' She smiled.

He went out without speaking and closed the door firmly behind him. He crossed the hall and opened the main door. Partridge stood there, grinning with boozy concentration.

'What the hell do you want?' Rayner said.

'You do sound short, dear boy. I have a message.'

He grinned wider.

'Well?'

'I'd better come inside. Somebody might be passing.'

'Let them pass! What is it?'

'It's from Garner,' said Partridge, quietly.

'What — !' Rayner stopped still. 'What the hell are you talking about? You're shot! You've been soaking it all the evening — '

'I had to be softened up before I could give the message,' Partridge said. 'You know what a sense of humour Garner had. Very sick.'

'Get on with it!'

'Well, old boy, it was one day when he was very bitter and twisted far beyond the normal, he said, 'If anything grave happens to me, wait a week and then ask Rayner what happened.' '

Rayner felt his head freeze and for a moment he could think of nothing to say as he glared at Partridge.

'You're further gone than usual!' he said at last. 'What on earth's the matter with you?'

'I'm telling you what the man said,' Partridge explained, awkwardly. 'It was his idea of a joke, but it happened to become quite topical. I thought I'd better tell you, in case he told somebody else the same thing. Quite frankly, Rayner, he made me promise. I'd drawn a bit ahead on my commission, so I promised.'

He looked round behind him.

'Well, there you are,' he said. 'I hope nobody did pass. Is the Hagworth here with you? If so, you'll feel better in the morning.' He grinned and went.

Rayner slammed the door and stood for a moment wondering what he should have done. Perhaps he should have treated it as a joke, but, by any standards, it was an insult, so perhaps he had reacted properly. A guilty man, perhaps, would have asked Partridge in and tried to get round him. Yes, perhaps he would have done just that. Keeping the hard, insulted line had certainly been the right thing.

He went back into the study.

'Not your lady,' Janet said, slyly.

There was no point in keeping quiet because Partridge and Janet would meet next day in the office.

'It was Partridge,' he said. 'Drunk.'

'What did he want — another drink?'

On the instant, as if by some kind of destructive instinct, or by the knowledge that she would certainly get to know, he told her.

She looked at the desk lamp and smiled, then shrugged.

'Well?' she said, looking up slowly. 'You did, didn't you? But that doesn't matter.' She went away from the desk and began, as he had, to pace the carpet. 'What does matter is how Garner *knew*. How he had it in his mind all that time that you would kill him in the end seems incredible. Yet, everything he did just before shows that he expected it.'

'So he set about composing puzzles for us, knowing that we would join forces?' he said.

'He knew I wouldn't care if he died. I didn't like him. Everything he did for me because of that. He fought an everlasting battle during his life to make me change from dislike to like — or at least, a subservient gratitude. He never got it.'

He sat on the arm of a chair, slowly and stared at her as if astonished.

'One damn surprise after another,' he said. 'Or are you lying?'

'I've no need of lying. I have done nothing wrong, I've nothing to cover up.' She stopped in front of him. 'Because I never liked him, he hated me. And he hated you. Yet he left the means of our having some sort of wealth if we could work it out. It could only be that he thought we were both villains.'

'Or it was something he felt was so clever he just had to believe that somebody would do it,' he said. 'As it is, the owner returns to Mallingford in June, so there are a few days before the place comes to life again. Garner couldn't have known that would be the case — '

'Or perhaps he knew the most likely

date when he might have an accident.'

He thought she began to smile, but the impression was fleeting. Rage flared up in him at her constant assumption that he had murdered Garner, and that she treated it as being without any consequence. Her suspicion was not new. He had felt it was there from that time by the graveside. Ever since then he had known she suspected — or even knew, as if she had been somewhere in the office that night.

The cold drench of fear at that thought damped down the rage in him. Until he thought, what difference would it make if she knew anyhow? If she had seen she had said nothing. How could she speak now? She would be an accomplice. She *was* an accomplice. His accomplice; his partner.

The partner he could never leave now without exchanging her for disaster.

'Pull yourself together,' she said, watching him. 'You must not show your feelings so much. In the circumstances, it wouldn't do any good.'

'Shut up,' he said.

She turned back to the desk.

'I'm sorry,' he said suddenly, and was surprised he had said it.

'One hundred hundred dollar bills,' she said. 'Whether genuine is not known to us. Therefore we cannot use them. Where did he get them?'

'How?' he said, getting up. 'You can't go into a bank and draw them.'

'It may be,' she said, 'that some items mean nothing in detail. The money. It seems to suggest this amount is negligible by comparison with what could be got if the puzzle is worked out. But the key — That might have a hole to fit it some way away from a case of razors.' She turned back to him. 'We'll have to get into Mallingford.'

'When we get in we'll have to do it,' he said. 'We can't afford a dummy run. We don't want to show up there at all.'

'We must,' she said.

★ ★ ★

Freddy sat back in his chair and stared at his secretary.

'Rayner? Good Lord!' He leant forward suddenly. 'Yes, of course. Show him in.'

She went up. He stood up. Rayner was shown in.

'It's nothing personal,' Rayner said, pausing as the door was closed behind him.

'That's all right. I'm glad you came in. Sit down. Cigarette?' Freddy sat back. 'Bit awkward, isn't it?' He grinned.

'This is a matter of clearing up some details of the Garner will,' Rayner said. 'I wondered if you knew who handled the Mallingford estate?'

'There's nothing to handle, old lad. It's not for sale, as far as I know, though I've heard there are private lets for very short periods, just to keep the place aired. The noble owner might not know of these. There is a housekeeper, but I have heard that she is absent a good deal while her employer is abroad, so it may not be easy to get in touch.'

'Well, I suppose she'd know if anyone had taken a short let there?'

'She would know. Probably the owner wouldn't.' Freddy sat back. 'I'm afraid

I was a bit overworked last night, old lad. I sort of bust things too soon. I apologise.'

Rayner sat solidly in his chair. 'It was disturbing,' he said, staring icily.

'I've said I'm sorry,' Freddy said, shortly, and looked at his desk. 'When I got back she'd gone.'

Rayner started a little. 'Left you?'

'Flat,' said Freddy. 'I don't like that sort of thing. It's inconclusive. You don't know when she might turn up again.' He paused, his eyes on his papers. 'I suppose you haven't seen her?'

'Is it likely? I was the one who forgot the bloody appointment.'

'You can't tell, with women,' Freddy said, shaking his head. 'They turn up when you think they won't just to create a little bit of hell for you . . . Why Mallingford?'

'Well, it seems he might have stayed there. The widow came to see me and asked if I could find out. I think she's after finding out what money he spent in the last couple of years, because he didn't leave any.'

'Quite a lot who seem well off don't leave much once the right mask is attached on the death bed. Pardon my lugube. I feel all flat and glum. Rows perish me. And this one's got all the loose ends in the air.'

'She may have gone to her mother,' Rayner said shortly, and got up. 'Well, thanks. I'll tell the widow there was nothing in it.'

'If Freda does turn up on your patch, will you let me know?' Freddy said.

'I will.'

He left and went back to his office. Partridge came to discuss the buying of a new line in bathroom carpets, and said nothing about the previous night.

'What are you going to do eventually?' Partridge said. 'Set up on your own, I suppose?'

'Eventually,' Rayner said. 'It needs my father's capital. He's getting a bit shy in his old age.'

'How old is he?'

'Sixty-four.'

'Oh well. I wish you luck anyhow.' Partridge went back to his own office.

An olive branch, Rayner thought; what's happened?

He had a number of callers during the day, and there was no convenient time to talk with Janet. Not that there was anything new to say, but his nervousness was becoming pervasive and sharing matters with her seemed to spread the load. Towards the end of the day he went into her office. She had gone early.

'She had a hair appointment,' Pat said in the outer office. 'I can deal with it, whatever it is.'

'It can wait till the morning,' he said. 'Don't worry.'

She watched him go with a faint smile of inner amusement.

As he turned back to his own room he looked back and saw a detective sergeant come in and have a word with Pat. She looked quite grave for a moment, as if the sergeant had told her something dreadful and exciting.

Rayner did not wait to see, but went to his own room.

He knew that detective-sergeant. He

had been around the offices when Garner's fatal accident was discovered. He had asked questions while keeping a friendly half smile on his face all the time. It had got to Rayner then, and he remembered it uneasily as he began to clear up his papers for the day.

He expected a knock at the door second by second. He was sure somebody had given him away. He wanted to go, and quickly, but he wanted much more to know what they were talking about in Mann's office. The police always went to the manager's office about little cases of shoplifting, obtaining goods by fraud and the other simple cases of determined forgetfulness.

Nothing happened. His papers were all put away, his desk clear, but still he stayed, watching his door as if wishing for the knock to come.

At last he decided to leave. In the outer office Pat was putting on her coat. He helped her on with it.

'What's with the law?' he said, in an odd tone.

'Oh, a dud cheque,' she said. 'Seems

it was stolen, anyhow. You'd think somebody who stole cheques would find out if the owner's got any money, wouldn't you? Came back 'RD' and when we asked the drawer he didn't know anything about it but the book had been reported stolen a month ago.'

'I suppose there are more knocking about somewhere,' Rayner said.

He went home. Mrs Colman had gone, leaving a note: 'Youngest poorly, must go. Your dinner's in bottom oven.'

He was relieved more than anything. At such a time he didn't want Mrs Colman bustling about. When women dusted they often opened drawers and had a gawp, just to pass the time.

He went into the study but did not open the bottom drawer. The Garner puzzle seemed to have become stupid, messy. Old socks. He supposed it was the socks which had put him off. Old socks, spiked with glue, cut with new holes and all the rest of it.

He poured himself a Scotch. The sergeant would not clear off the back of his neck. He could almost feel the man behind him, with that penetrating, friendly grin, saying 'You didn't kill Garner, old man, now, did you? I mean, its laughable, isn't it? The whole idea, I mean — '

Perhaps the sergeant would even laugh.

Rayner went back to the desk and took out the photographs only, leaving the rest of the distasteful muck in the drawer. Once again he spread out the prints and again he studied the backgrounds.

He began darting his eyes from one to another some prints away, then back, then jazzing from side to side, almost making a moving picture of it. He stood up to get better length and repeated the exercise.

Janet was right. Picking out the pictures oddly made the figures look as if they were doing a kind of dance against a moving panorama of the great house interior.

He went to the light and snapped it on, then closed the window curtains. Back at the desk he stood looking down at the photographs, then passed his hand edgewise in a fanning movement between his eyes and the prints. The figures began to take on curious shapes and suddenly they made a Y, then further off, an N, then, against the white stone edge of a fireplace, an E.

He went no further. He knew if he did he would see his own name spelt out. The letters were crude, perhaps uncertain because by the very nature of their forming, they had to be, but there was no doubt that careful study at a police laboratory would find his name there.

He crossed to a corner of the room and poured another Scotch. He drank some, then pulled back the curtains.

The first black shock was lifting. Janet had shown a way, a method of finding a word; perhaps his own name was no more than an extension of that.

Why imagine that it had been done to name him as a murderer? In the first place it was impossible for Garner to have known at any time before his death. He may have had suspicions, but then, he had been suspicious of many people.

No. The careful placing, timing and

direction of the film session could have been nothing to do with murder, or the fear of it. It had been carefully planned as a code in case anything happened to him before he could act.

Rayner went back to the table and placed the pictures in the spelling order, Y, N, E. The A he already knew from Janet; indicating the fanlight once more. But with that set out in spelling order, there was no order in the pictures, no sequence that he could see.

The phone rang. For a moment he thought he should stow away the prints quickly in case the caller should see and know what he was trying to do. The instant passed. He answered.

'We go to Mallingford tomorrow afternoon,' Janet said. 'I have paid a gardener for his absence and a back door key. Right?'

'Right. By the way, did you have your hair done?'

'Odd question. Yes.'

She rang off.

As he put the phone down a new angle on Garner's weird action over

Mallingford came to him.

Supposing that Garner had found he had an incurable disease, that was bound to kill him? Supposing he feared not Rayner, but disease? A tumour on the brain, perhaps. He probably would not have told anyone unless it could have hurt them. He had not been a man to share anything, not even miseries. All his life at the firm had been for the firm, or that was the impression he had given. Perhaps that was why he had got on so well. He had been a two-life man; one in the office, another when he left.

Rayner finished his drink, then went and rang Janet's number.

'What doctor did he go to?' he asked.

'I don't remember that he ever went. He used to take aspirin quite a bit, and other patents likewise. He got headaches, yes. What are you on to? Do you mean he was scatty?'

'Well, this business isn't sane, is it? The hole in the sock routine is vicious, but it's directed against somebody he thought wouldn't see it; his widow. His will remembered everybody he hated.'

'Correct. But he hated everybody. I wonder why you don't understand that.'

'It doesn't matter. I'm just beginning to wonder whether it's worth going further. Is something there, or is this just a fool-making puzzle?'

'There is something to be discovered,' she said, and rang off.

He poured another Scotch.

What was the matter with him? Surely, it had been a good day. The bats of hell had faded. Partridge had made peace. Freddy had made peace. Janet was on his side. Who was against him now? Only Freda. Did Freda matter? Only to his cowardice.

And the real meaning of Garner foreseeing his death. How could he have expected to be murdered, and by a specific person who had no reason to do it? Clearly it indicated knowledge of another kind; that Death was there, in his head anyway, and he knew how long it would stay its' hand.

It fitted with the headaches, the crazy puzzles, the vast, meticulous care he had taken to set the film, employ the filmers,

157

the participants, the pilot, the posing of the actors — it was all crazy, whichever way you looked at it. No sane person would ever conceive such a plan, unless as a great memorial to himself and his cleverness.

At that time, Rayner found it easy to penetrate the criminal mind. He found it easy to penetrate the egotist, the poseur. He found it almost simple to explore the devious mind, the twisted mind.

But he did not know that the mind of a madman is away from the world of evaluation and calculation, and is of itself sublime, above the device of the coward, which, in fact, is all that Rayner really was.

8

Rayner was beginning to worry about everything. He was unpleasantly aware of it. He knew that he no longer trusted anything or anyone, and felt he had to be on continual guard.

And the reason for the increasing uneasiness was not the living people around him, but the dead one; Garner. The idea of Banquo which had floated in and out of his head at the beginning of the Janet association, had been replaced by an almost solid figure of Garner, standing behind him, laughing.

However crazy Garner had been, there was never absent from his mind the need for making money out of everything. The pictures taken at Mallingford had been covered, without any doubt, by selling them in conjunction with the photographer, as Janet had said.

He had been salting money from the tills for years without anyone knowing — anyone that is, but Rayner. It was only a small thing he had seen one evening, when leaving late that had started his suspicion of Garner's extractions. But for that he would never have rumbled it at all.

Could that established keen but careful love of money have any bearing on the problem of the legacy? They had used his deviousness, his weird humour, his lasciviousness and the rest to try and solve the puzzle, but never once had they considered his greed for money.

Yet here in the legacy was a stack of American money.

And then another idea came to his mind. N, Y, E had seemed to be made by the actions of the figures. He had taken them, rearranged them to spell the middle of his name, but shuffled again, they made Yen.

The A which he had taken in as well had been wrongly taken in, because it had come from a different system they had forged, of numbering letters.

He turned impatiently from looking at the desk. It was absurd, the idea of making the players look like letters, anyhow. It could only be done by tricking the eyesight and splitting vision.

He was getting too absorbed, too close to the problem, almost as an escape from thinking of the encroaching world of danger surrounding him.

Even he thought that his mind rejected the idea fiercely. Why did he think that everyone was suspecting him? Why should he imagine they suspected him now, when they hadn't at the death and just after it? The inquest had decided on accidental death. The matter was ended. He alone was bringing it up.

He poured another drink.

Tomorrow, to Mallingford. He did not think it wise, even if she had got rid of the gardener, because somebody might later find out about the gardener.

But still, it wouldn't be the day of the robbery.

He began to walk about the room, glass in hand. Suppose there was nothing for them at Mallingford? Suppose the whole puzzle had been part of an elaborate joke, designed to get them into trouble?

That made him angry. He had thought of it before and put it out of his mind. His trouble was becoming a confusion, so that he could not remember exactly how he had refuted his fears before and so suffered them again and again.

He went back to the desk and studied the backgrounds, the scenes of the house in the pictures. Tomorrow he would be there.

★ ★ ★

He drove her in his car. The entrance to the grounds lay down a private lane. On either side of the open gates there were high brick walls which seemed to enclose the estate.

'Stop here,' she said. 'I'll get out. Bear in mind that the gates and all the other entrances will be shut and locked when we make the grab. I must find a way over in daylight while you follow the clues in the house. We don't want to stay more than an hour. That's the period I arranged.'

She got out.

162

'Are you coming in later?' he said. His voice felt dry and harsh, grating in his throat.

'No. My job's outside. We'll be helpless if we don't find a way over the wall. Yours shouldn't take too long. Don't forget; keep your gloves on.'

'I'm not likely to forget!' he snapped and drove off into the grounds.

Near the front of the house he turned off the drive into a branch screened by high hedges, then stopped and got out.

Birds sang now and again up in the trees. That was all he could hear as he walked back, round the end of the hedge and approached the front door, by walking on the grass beside the drive.

The door and fanlight were familiar to him and he felt as if he had been there before. He went to the door, turned the big iron handle and pushed. The heavy door swung inwards silently. He walked into the familiar hall and closed the door behind him.

He stood for a whole minute looking round. It was all exactly as the prints showed, but much smaller than he had thought. He turned to the panelling beside the door frame and felt the wood. A panel swung open quite easily, showing a switch inside with two buttons, one marked with a red dot. He closed the panel and went to the stairs.

There again, the opening panel in the staircase side was easy to see. He pressed the wooden knob and pulled the panel open. Inside was a box with no lid. Two rows of eight porcelain fuses showed with a chart above them, showing which circuits were controlled. A large lever switch at the end of the fuses obviously controlled the main supply. He closed the panel.

The corridor led off to the right of the stairs and parallel with them so that the passage entrance pointed to one side of the front door.

He went into the corridor, carefully watching the wall on the stair side.

It was then that, for the first time since coming in, he had a feeling that someone was watching. He looked each way, stepped to the hall and looked all round, then up the stairs. He listened.

The quiet was almost oppressive.

He decided it was his nerves kicking, which were creating sensations of being watched, even being followed.

He went on searching the panels on the staircase side of the corridor but could find no trace of any opening as indicated by the hole —

The spiked hole in the sock. A hole in the bloody *sock*! What the hell was he doing here, following a trail laid by anything so sordid and stupid as a hole in a bloody sock?

He began to lose his temper and would have left then, but he realised in time that while he was close, it would be foolish not to see the big room which was, presumably the final grotto.

He opened a wide door in the opposite wall of the corridor from the one he had searched. The room inside was as he had seen it in the photographs, even the furniture was in the same positions.

He stood in the middle of the room and let his rage subside enough for him to remember that somewhere right close to him at that moment was the treasure which Garner had hoped to have for himself.

He closed the door. With that done, the silent peace of the big, cool room soothed his nerves. He knew that this was his opportunity to clear the way for the removal of what might be a fortune. If he could trace it now, the final act would be easy. It was a pity that, through Janet making the arrangement with the gardener, he could not take it now, but it would be suicide to do so when the pointer to the thief would be so clear.

He began a careful search of the panelled wall behind the big sofa, and again, found no obvious cracks or means of creating an opening by sliding some loose part. Of course, the panelling was old and there were cracks and uneven joints here and there, and he pushed and pulled and tried to slide parts of the structure, but nothing gave.

He went back and tried to get into the position from which he thought the shots had been taken, and lined up one corner of the sofa back as he remembered it, pointing to the third panel on the third line up from the side of the door.

He pushed the panel, tried the mouldings all round it and at last placed his gloved hand flat on it and tried to move it sideways. It went quite easily to the left.

A safe, circular, like the breech of a gun, showed there. There was no keyhole, but a handle and a combination dial marked with numbers up to twenty-six.

A curiously marked dial, but it excited Rayner. Twenty-six was the number of the prints, the alphabet. He turned the dial experimentally. It turned very easily, almost as if it was doing nothing at all during its revolutions, just freewheeling.

He slid the panel to and left the house. When he got back to where he had left Janet, she was not there. He pulled on to the grass amongst the edge of a wood running alongside the wall and got out.

She came up from along the wall on the other side, of the gates, so he did not see her until he turned and looked over the car roof. He opened the door for her when she came round the car.

'Okay?' she said.

'Okay,' he affirmed. He went round and got in. 'Find a way?'

'You'll have to climb a tree,' she said. 'A branch reaches the top of the wall. Stout. Don't worry. You'll need a track suit.'

'I haven't one.'

'Buy one. They make things easier, quite obviously.'

'You may be right,' he said angrily. 'How high do I climb?'

'You've seen the wall. That high.'

'Cow,' he said.

'What was it? A safe?'

'Yes. Combination Twenty-six numbers all in.'

'Oh. So now we look for a combination amongst the alien porn. Ah well. Garner was never easy.'

'He was mad!'

'You sound convinced.'

'Well, whose safe is it? How did he know the combination? Was it he who put whatever it is into the safe? If so what for? Why use somebody else's safe for your ill-gotten gains?'

'What exactly do you mean by that?' she said, calmly, but very precisely.

He realised he had made another mistake.

'I'm following on in suggesting he had something he hid there,' he said.

'You are following on your suggestion made before, about him milking the tills. Where did you get that idea from? He didn't live loudly.'

'All right, what do I mean, then?' he shouted.

'You mean your nerves are becoming shattered into a lot of little pieces,' she said. 'We'd better get this over soon now, before you blow the whole thing.'

She looked out of the window on her side and smiled where he could not see her.

★ ★ ★

Next day, Sunday, Janet phoned him at six am. He was dazed with a hangover, and when he woke he shook slightly as he reached for the phone on the side table.

'Come over,' she said.

169

'Get stuffed!' he said.

'I'll be waiting.' She rang off.

He put back the phone. Fury evaporated. Fear returned. What was she after? What had happened?

He got up. What had happened? After sloshing his face in cold water he asked it again. What had happened? What could have happened? They hadn't done anything. Not yet. Or had something come out about him?

He looked in a mirror, thought he looked awful and had a shower. He dressed in slacks and wool shirt and went downstairs. The curtains were still drawn in the study. He hated that. It was like somebody dead. Old people did that when somebody died. Kept out the daylight. Stayed in the frightened gloom, the cold misery.

He pulled the curtains aside and found the whisky decanter. With it in hand he turned and saw the prints still spread out across the desk. She was there, arrogant, splendid, beautiful —

His hands almost crushed the cut glass decanter. 'Beautiful? What the hell!

170

Beautiful? She was ugly! Her features were ugly, ugly, ugly! But the body — the body — that was beautiful, but the face, the mind, the soul — they were ugly!

He shut his eyes. The rage subsided after a few seconds. He turned and put the endangered decanter back on the cabinet shelf.

He realised that things were going awry, because he was refusing to recognise certain facts. He was involved in trying to find a small fortune, perhaps the sum of Garner's petty pilfering over the years. Perhaps that was the secret of the safe in the big house.

He was involved with Janet; she had told him nothing of what she really knew, and he had mentally fought her all the time, getting no help because he was acting the stubborn fool. He should have gone about it in quite another way. It would not have been that distasteful.

He could have had full co-operation from her, instead he had held off, let prejudice and fear pull him from the way that any sane man would have taken at the start.

He went out into the kitchen and made tea, and kept thinking; beautiful, how had such a word come into his head? Perverseness? Self-irritation? How had it come into his head? Why hadn't he laughed and let it go out again?

Because he couldn't.

'Shut up! Shut up!' he shouted aloud as if to some irritating creature zig-zagging in the air of the room.

He stood quite stiffly for a moment, then relaxed and poured some tea. He sat down and sipped it. He had to be calm, stop this stupid perversity, control his sudden rages or soon he would be as mad as Garner.

Garner. As he thought of him he could feel that fat neck in his hand again, pulling it back and then smashing it down on the safe edge. He hadn't gripped hard. Garner had been almost flaccid, as if expecting and agreeing to that final assault.

The hot tea began to soothe him. He could relive that scene without being frightened, enjoying the same confidence and coolness as he had at the time.

He had had the feeling of satisfying something within him far more than the greed for money which had begun the crime.

He ate some cold ham and his spirits began to recover and rise out of the depths of sudden fears and night pictures of Garner's death. Outside a grey morning began to change to bright sunlight.

When he set out for the flats, anxiety returned. He went back into the study, and put the things back in the bottom drawer of the desk, taking a last look right through the prints before he put them down with the rest of the items.

As he closed the drawer he realised he had not looked at anything in the prints but Janet. Scene after scene he had looked at Janet. He had not looked for the fanlight, the alarm box, the fuse box, the safe wall, but at Janet. He stood up and kicked the shut drawer.

He was coming under an influence. She was a witch. That was it; a witch. The body beautiful with the mind of evil.

When she opened the door to him she wore a plain silk dressing gown, and walked away from him, the stuff shimmering over her back, leaving him to close the door.

'What's happened?' he said, following.

She made as if to look over her shoulder, then changed her mind and walked on.

'What's happened?' he said again, more sharply.

She walked across the split-level room and into a big bedroom. By the bed she stopped and turned.

'Why did you ring? What's happened?' he said.

'Nothing's happened,' she said, untying the gown. 'I want a man. I fancy you just now. Get your clothes off. We can talk things over more easily.' She slipped off the gown and got gracefully into the bed. 'Come — get rid of your murderous inhibitions, your suicidal introspection.' She smiled.

Very slowly, he undressed, watching her all the time. She smiled and said nothing. He thought she could have said,

'I knew you'd have to come,' but she said nothing; just smiled.

About half past ten there was a ringing at the front door. She donned the silk gown again and went out to answer, leaving the bedroom door slightly ajar. He sat up and listened.

From the hall across the split level room he heard her say, 'Mrs Garner. I am surprised.'

'There is something I wanted to talk to you about. I won't be long. I'm on my way to church.'

'Come in.'

He heard them come into the room next door. Alarm bells began to drive the calm out of his head, but he had no idea why.

'Well, Mrs Garner?' Janet said.

'I have had a very extraordinary phone call. Anonymous. It sounded like the girl who used to put my husband's calls through from the office, but I couldn't be sure of that, so don't think about it.'

'As you like, Mrs Garner. The call?'

'Well, yes. The girl said my husband was murdered for money, and that money was taken at the same time.'

'The money in the safe agreed with all the books and accounts, Mrs Garner. The police went into all that, you know.'

'Yes. But these calls are very disturbing and I thought that you, being the secretary — my husband's secretary would know whether any money could have been taken and covered up?'

'If it was, Mrs Garner, where was it, whose was it, and who brought it there? And if it was stolen why hadn't the money from the safe gone, too? It was thirteen thousand pounds, you know.'

'Yes, I know. I just wanted to satisfy my mind. The call upset me.'

'It sounds like somebody trying to stir up trouble for a particular person,' said Janet firmly. 'Did it name anyone?'

'Mr Rayner. I don't believe anything of him, but that is the name she said ought to be — investigated — the man, not the name, of course.'

'You are suggesting that our receptionist made this call, accusing one of our senior staff members of murder and robbery?'

'No, no, not exactly — '

'Our receptionist would never make such a call at any time, for any reason, Mrs Garner. We are a closely knit staff in that office and discuss together any matters which may affect us all.

'So, Mrs Garner, I know, for instance, that you called on Mr Rayner asking him about me, and you called on me, asking me about him. I don't believe there was any phone call. I believe that someone is putting you up to something which you haven't the guile or strength to carry out. Take my advice; go away and in future take care what you say or you may find yourself in a court facing a charge of criminal libel. Good morning, Mrs Garner. Go on to church and pray for better guidance in the future.'

'You bitch! You slinky bloody whore! You got his — '

'Get out, Mrs Garner. Or do you want me to throw you out?'

There were no further words until Janet said, 'Good morning, Mrs Garner. It was nice of you to call and give your game away.'

He heard the front door close with

a well-oiled click. She came back into the bedroom. He was standing at the window, watching the river and turned.

'I hope you heard,' she said.

'Yes. She's barmy.'

'No, she's still trying to find out where the money is. She thinks we know. Someone is putting her up to making these visits, which even she must begin to see are looking fishy to us. So someone is pushing her forward. Probably the woman she lives with.'

She turned and shoved him backwards on to the bed before he knew what was happening. She joined him there.

'I wish I hadn't been born so curious,' she said, smiling again. 'Never mind. It's forgotten.'

At twelve the bell rang again.

'Great Scott! She's back again!' Janet said.

Once more she put on the silk gown and went out, tying it about her. Again he went to the partly open door and listened.

'Partridge! What the hell are you doing here?' Janet said.

'Let me in, Janet. I am distrait. That bloody woman keeps getting on to me.'

'Come in,' Janet said, irritably. They came into the lounge. 'What bloody woman?'

'The Garner relict. I think she's going round the bend. She's got some fix about Rayner murdering her husband for some money that wasn't there. I don't know. She came this morning and tried to shove me into going to the police. I ask you! What the hell for? He fell on the safe. You know he'd been getting these dizzy spells. I wonder that didn't come out. But I don't suppose they want to string these things out. Gosh! you look luscious in that, Janet.'

'She came here as well,' Janet said. 'Is she visiting round the staff, trying to work up something against Rayner? What for? What can she get out of it?'

'Search me. But she did let slip something about what Margaret said — I think that's the name of the woman Garner said she ran off with. It was a Margaret, wasn't it?'

'I think it was. She may be being put

179

up to it. She's stupid enough. And she runs out of argument, then goes, but then comes back with another one. It is as if she goes out to refuel from Margaret and then comes back in again.'

'She's got to be weak in the head.'

'The best thing, really, is to make her go to the police. They'll take the flea out of her ear for her.'

'Oh no, no police,' said Partridge sharply. 'That leaves a bit of a smell all round. No police.'

9

Rayner stood still and listened, hardly daring to breathe in case he missed a word implicating himself.

'No police,' Partridge repeated. 'That isn't the way at all.'

'Then what is?' Janet said.

'Laugh her off or scare her off,' he said, firmly. 'If she's allowed to go on like this she'll involve everybody in the bloody office, sooner or later. I like the job. I'm not backing out because of some butch baroness stirring things up and sending in the tame mouthpiece.'

'She's not that tame. Don't under-estimate her.'

'Well, lesser, then. She's dead set on the Rayner idea, that he did it, and that he got something out of it. Well, there wasn't anything in the office taken that night, and his legacy of old socks and pretty pictures couldn't have been anything but a smack in the face, like my wine that he'd drunk, and the golf clubs. Here, dear,' he said, bringing the little bag of clubs out of his pocket. 'Something else to remember him by.'

He put the bag of clubs on a coffee table. She looked at it for a moment.

'And what else?' she said.

'Oh, she said you owned the flats, in fact,' he said. 'That's probably why she's given up the idea of fighting you for them. But the point is, Janet, she's after something, she and the woman behind her, and they're not going to give up until either they're convinced there's nothing to gain or they're scared to go on.'

'But if we try and scare them it will show we're guilty of something. It's not worth that risk of starting gossip about ourselves when in fact we haven't done anything. You know the smoke without fire routine. You don't want to start that, do you?'

'No. On the other hand, I'm getting fed up with it. I'm being forced into something I have nothing to do with, made to feel guilty when I've done nothing.'

'That's the kind of woman she is; a natural-born irritant. Forget her. Show her the door.'

'Maybe, maybe,' he said, turning and walking uneasily a few paces, then back again. 'I don't know what's best to do. I've got the feeling now that there really was something Garner left, and nobody's rumbled it.'

'If you believe that, I wish you luck.'

'It's just that I can't see how he spent his pay, bonuses and all the rest if he left nothing at the end.'

'He had secrets; haven't we all?'

'What the hell did he spend it on, then? He got rent from you. He would hardly have paid you while you were paying rent through his lawyers — Oh, I've made a bad faux pas. Sorry.'

She laughed.

'Don't apologise. I'm used to being called a whore. I suppose I look the part. Now you go along and forget this woman. You're building her up into something she isn't.'

'Okay. If you think that's best, willco.'

He went. Rayner came out of the bedroom.

'He didn't come because of the woman,' he said, angrily. 'He's after something on his own account. He even said there might be something nobody knows about.'

'Don't get upset,' she said, and lit a cigarette. 'He could be a nuisance, but he did say something that clicked in my head like a switch.'

'Let's have a drink,' he said, going to a table by the window. 'What clicked?'

'The idea that Garner might have wanted to involve all the office staff in a scandal if he died.'

He looked round in surprise. 'Yes, he could have done a thing like that. But there again comes this idea with it; that he knew he was going to die. How?'

'The only answer I've been able to think of is that he had done something which he felt would make somebody do him in. Leave that: it may come out when we know the rest of it.

'Go back to my click. You got the main puzzle, but suppose it isn't complete?

Suppose Partridge got a part and Mann, also. Suppose we've been wrong all the time, trying to get at a numbers system to solve the thing, when in fact, it could be cards.'

'Get on.' He had a drink but kept his eyes on her as if watching for traces of a lie to show.

'Clubs,' she said, with a gesture towards the little bag on the coffee table. 'Now the actor with me in those flicks called himself Espada, which is Spanish for a sword of some sort, but which we have changed to spades for the card suit — '

'And hearts, I suppose, is represented by the whole sequence,' he suggested, sarcastically.

She went back to the bedroom.

'We'll go back and see those prints again. I have a feeling now it could read much easier than it's seemed to up to now. Diamonds might be what he hid in the safe.'

'It can't be as simple as that,' he said. 'But you can't tell with a crackpot.' He finished the drink.

At the house, with the prints spread out again, it did seem somehow simpler, as if it should all now be easy to read.

'There,' she pointed to a picture near the end where the actor's head exactly obscured the safe panel. 'Spade,' she said, and wrote down the sequence in numbers, saying them as she did it, '1916145. We'll try that on the safe lock tonight.'

'What?' he cried, in alarm. 'But we're not ready! We couldn't — '

'We must do it now. Partridge is already nosing around and if there's something still to be found, he'll find it. He's the sort. Worries like a terrier. We'll go tonight. After that, all this must be destroyed.'

'It could be dead wrong,' he said. 'It's so damned easy now. Just that. The clubs. But what about the dollars, and Mann's chair? What was the point of that?' He glared at her.

'You know the point of that,' she said, eyeing him with a cool, amused look. 'It has a false seat. You can hide things in it.'

'Funny the police didn't spot it,' he said, turning away.

'They were only looking at the result of an accident,' she said. 'And *you* told them everything they wanted to know.'

'One of these days I'll get you round the neck and screw your bloody head off!' he shouted.

'Now look!' she shouted back, so that her violence shocked him into silence. 'You've got to learn to control yourself,' she went on quietly. 'These out-bursts will finish you, otherwise. How can you tell what you'll let out in the middle of a stupid temper? Hold yourself back, otherwise you'll find yourself in for life.'

'I'm sorry;' he almost shouted again, but just stopped short of it.

'You're not really that scared, are you? Shouldn't have thought you'd get nerves like that. Anyhow, as you've got 'em, hold 'em.'

'Okay, okay, right!' he said shortly. 'You jumped on the clubs as the key for cards. I remember you said the actor's name before. It didn't mean anything to me. Hearts, yes. I remember that, too.

It just all seems too damned easy for a twisted mind like his.'

'Not twisted. Over-elaborate. He cut out old time-tables as a puzzle for a place name. Then the old sock idea and the pictures. We tried different systems with them, and now the clubs click in.'

'But why? Why? Why go to all that trouble for *himself*?' he said, pacing. 'He knew the combination, where the safe was and what was in it! How could he be so sure he would die? Accident. Yes. Partridge says dizzy spells. Yes. No known doctor visits, but he could have gone away and got a short-term ticket. How did he keep quiet about that? If it was that which convinced him he'd die.'

'It must have been something like that,' she said. 'All he did points to the fact he was sure of death.'

'If I knew how he felt that I wouldn't bother about the rest of it. Tonight?' He looked at her. 'It's too soon.'

'I feel we're being pushed. Partridge, the widow and the woman behind her. Garner must have spread something before he died. He must have dealt round some sort of idea there was something to be found when he died. I keep feeling that.'

'Once we've got it and chucked all this into the incinerator, it won't matter.'

He looked at her sharply. 'You didn't arrange anything with the caretaker or anything like that?'

'That would be traceable afterwards. The way I collared the gardener is because he lives near the town and does my garden in his odd hours. Nobody will be at Mallingford tonight. That's clear. The owner will be back sooner than expected — next weekend, so this one they have a last fling.' She watched him. 'You needn't worry. I have the facts right.'

'If you say — ' he said doubtfully.

'Do you really think we could wait, now these people are fussing around us?'

'No. No, it wouldn't be wise to wait. I have to agree. I only hope the prize is worth it in the end.'

'Another bloody depression,' Janet said.

'I'm beginning to think Garner wasn't the only barmy one. Going by my friends, I could qualify. Though why I should call you my friend I can't think. I forget who, but someone said mutual hatred is more stimulating and lasting than a close friendship.'

'And someone else said all things are subject to change,' Rayner said, bitterly. 'And when it changes, it loses.'

'Cynics come and go,' she said. 'It would be best for us to go away from the town today. It's fine. It'll take our minds off things, and further, it'll cause no fuss about anyone wondering tomorrow where we were today.'

'You could be right,' he said sourly. 'You've obviously worked it all out. But how — so suddenly — ' He shrugged.

'Something clicks, there's an answer. It may not be the right one, but I feel it's close enough to lead to the right one.'

'I shall not go in alone,' he said, slowly, very firmly.

'You bet you won't,' she said. 'I'll be right by you when you crack that safe.' She began to clear the legacy from the desk.

★ ★ ★

She wanted to be driven back to the flat first, but on the way, changed her mind and directed him to the pub where he had met Freddie that night.

'Why there?' he said irritably.

'To get them to make some sandwiches we can take with us, and leave a false scent,' she said.

This was done without talking to anyone but the barmaid. Janet explained she was going to see a cottage belonging to an aunt who was away, and on which she was keeping an eye. It was enough to start any curious person on several gossipy tracks.

From the pub they went back to the flats and drove round to the garages at the side. They left Rayner's car and she drove a car out of her garage which Rayner had not seen before. He got in with her.

'Where did you get this?'

'Hired it.'

'Bloody old battleaxe, isn't it?'

'It's not noticeable. That's the thing. There's a case on the back floor with torches and anything we might need. I got it ready for whenever we decided to go.'

'And what if the hearts, clubs and spades are all wrong?'

'We should have all night to try a variety of combinations suggested by his clues.'

'We're rushing it too fast. All of a sudden — today, just because of the clubs — there's something wrong.'

'We'll find out what it is when we get there,' she said.

She drove away to the north-west, passing Mallingford ten miles to the east, on a system of by-roads. She drove into a wood and stopped to have the sandwiches twenty miles north west of the night's target.

They walked through the wood and found a stream. They sat on rocks and watched the water, and thin, fresh green thickening on the trees, tinged with gold from the shafts of sunlight.

'Oh God,' he said, in a strange voice. He stared into the water.

'What's the matter?' she said, watching him sharply.

He seemed to drag himself out of a dream.

'I suddenly had a dreadful feeling I might never see anything like this again — after tonight,' he said, and looked at her for a moment. 'Don't worry. It's the madness you keep talking about. Nothing to bother about.'

'Tell me,' she said, quietly, 'what did you mean to do with your life? You had ambitions. I guess you came into the firm to keep your father quiet. But how did you buckle down the way you did?'

'Because I'm not strong enough to do what I meant to do,' he said. 'Because I'm weak in all senses, mostly moral. I haven't the fibre. Up till a few days ago I still meant to chuck it and get into something I could crash value and walk out with the proceeds.'

'Your tempers are rage against yourself for this weakness,' she said, and shrugged, 'but the trouble could easily be that you could be what you want if you had somebody who believed in you, no matter what sort of a sod you were. But you have no chance of having anyone while you just kick everybody away.'

'You've got it wrong,' he said. 'Somewhere, you're wrong.' He tossed pebbles into the stream. 'I don't know what it is you've got wrong, but it is.'

'You must get rid of this feeling by tonight,' she said.

'It was just a passing moment, a feeling.'

'Someone walking over your grave. Everyone gets it.'

★ ★ ★

In the early evening they called at a pub ten miles north of Mallingford. They talked to the barman asking what the neighbourhood was like in the manner of those thinking of buying a property roundabout.

She then drove north seven miles and called into a second pub. There she asked much the same questions. At nine they left, heading west, then turned down towards Mallingford keeping to by roads. It was then dark.

'You've mugged up the maps pretty thoroughly,' he said.

'It seemed wise.'

They came to the edge of the wood which ran along the south wall of the estate. She drove into a track off the road and stopped when she was sure the car could no longer be seen by anyone passing on the road.

They got out.

'Got your gloves?'

'Yes.'

'Remember this. If Garner did use that safe for his own stuff, then no one is going to miss it later.'

'You believe that he did have something valuable after all?'

'What else did he do with all the money he filched?' she said, as they walked away together, she carrying a small torch and he the bag she had prepared.

'You admit it at last,' he said.

'I know he fiddled, perhaps a lot; how much, I wouldn't know. I do know that I never had any of it, nor did his wife. There might have been another woman. That's always possible.'

She stopped and made a brief flash of the torch at a tree just ahead of them.

'That's the one,' she said 'In the bag there's a rope. I've knotted it at intervals to make it simpler. Sling it over the branch up there. I'll flash a light when you cast.'

He brought out the rope, found one end, which was looped.

'You've thought of everything,' he said, sourly. 'Okay. Shine.'

She pointed the torch beam up to the branch. He cast the noosed end of the rope up to the branch. It went over the branch then came back and dropped again.

'Not enough slack,' he said, and tried again. He missed entirely. The third time the noose went over and dropped down the other side of the branch.

She zipped the bag. 'I'll chuck it up to you.'

He began to clamber up the rope. But for the knots he felt he could not have done it. He reached the branch.

'Right,' he said. 'Throw. Don't use a light. I can see enough.'

She tossed the bag four times before he could catch it.

'Right,' she said. 'Get on the wall. I'm coming up.'

He reached the wall easily. It was a matter of three or four feet, no more. He watched her shadowy figure climb the rope. She was agile, as if she had practised somewhere. They joined on the wall top, which was formed by a plain stone coping.

From the top they could see the great square mass of the house, a grey ghost in the May night light.

'Drop,' she said. 'It's ten feet.' As she spoke she pulled the rope along the branch and let it hang down on the inside of the wall.

He tossed the bag down, then dropped. The soil was soft from winter rains drying in the spring. She dropped beside him, staggered and fell back against the wall before she got her balance.

'Right,' she said.

He took up the bag. They walked silently towards the house on springy turf. At the white front door he stopped and looked up at the fanlight.

'Okay,' she said. 'Stand against the reveal of the door. I'm climbing up on you.'

He felt relieved, nodded and stood where he was told.

'Give me a stirrup,' she said.

He did that. She lifted herself by one foot with her hands on his head, then scrambled up him until she stood with her flat heeled shoes on his shoulders. He heard her shift the fanlight inwards.

'Hold my ankles,' she whispered. 'I'm going to reach in and down the inside of the door. Hold tight.'

He did as he was told. He was amazed at her agility, her capacity to do almost anything a man, such as he, would have managed to do. She was big, too, and yet seemed to move with the suppleness of a boy.

He felt her legs begin to rise and

grasped the ankles tightly as she strained to reach the alarm box inside. Then she stood on his shoulders again.

'Right,' she said, breathing a little hard, and came down clumsily, shoving him against the door as she came.

'Why wasn't the fanlight wired?' he said when she was down. 'I don't understand that.'

'Garner. He knew it was never opened officially, so he made sure it did unofficially. Don't forget your benefactor. He gave it all to you.' She laughed very quietly. 'Now the door and the key.'

She brought a small wallet from an inside pocket of her jacket and from it, took a key.

'Where did you get a key?' he said.

'It's the key to the box of razors,' she said.

'It's too small!' he hissed.

'There is more than one way of using a key,' she said, and began probing the keyhole with the small key. 'I had a husband, once, it turned out he was a jewel thief, a Parisian who bragged about his exploits as a way of making me unhappy, because he knew I was scared he would be caught. He was a bastard, a true Apache — ' she paused.

He held his breath.

'Got it?' he whispered, after a few seconds.

'I thought I had,' she said. 'I divorced him when I was twenty and he was just starting ten years in the jug — in Paris, that is, which is a little harder than here — Hang on!'

Both waited tensely, as, very slowly, she turned the big handle. When it was fully over, she pushed.

The door came open.

Both let out little sighs of relief and stood for a moment breathing in deeply before they went into the hall.

'Get the plugs out,' she said, and bolted the front door. 'Just in case anyone calls, or there's some other alarm system.'

He went to the staircase side and did as she said, using a big torch from the bag for the purpose. He pulled all the fuse bars out and put them on the floor below the open panel, then pulled down the main switch.

'Bloody antiquated, I should think,' he said. 'The alarm system. I reckon it must be just one that sets gongs going and frightens people away.'

She went by without apparently listening to him and entered the corridor. He got up and followed her till she stopped and shone her torch beam on to the opposite wall.

'I wonder what was indicated up there?' she said.

'There's nothing,' he said. 'I tried every panel. Nothing.'

She turned and opened the door into the big room. The four large windows showed clearly against the grey light of the night. Using her torch carefully so as not to show outside, she pulled the curtains, one after the other.

He turned to the wall and counted the panels up from the skirting and across from the door. As she finished with the curtains and joined him, he slid the panel across and exposed the safe.

'It's too easy,' he breathed, almost to himself. 'Too easy! Something's wrong somewhere.'

'Hold on,' she said in a soft voice, and reached into the breast pocket where she had kept the key. She brought out a piece of paper. 'I'll read out the numbers.'

She noticed he was holding his gloved hands together just below the safe. His hands were trembling.

10

'Okay?' she said, looking up at him from the line of figures.

He clenched his shaking hands together tightly, then let go. He nodded.

'Right,' he said, and turned to the safe.

She looked from him to the bright circle of the safe, and held her torch so that she could both see the paper and shine the edge of the beam at the safe. She began to read.

The gloved fingers trembled so that at the third turn of the dial he stood back a little and gripped his hands together hard.

'Bloody cramp!' he muttered.

She waited without speaking. Shamed, he went back to the dial. She went on reading the numbers. Once more his hands shook so that he had to stop and crush them together.

'Did you shake like that when you

killed him?' she said quietly.

'No.' He answered tonelessly, as if even his anger was lost in the spasms of fear shaking his body.

Again she waited in silence, eyes on the safe, as if seeing what was behind that little round door. He steadied and put his hands to the dial again.

'This sequence might not be the right one,' she said. 'You must be prepared for that.'

'I know! Shut up!' He turned the last number, then seemed to hesitate, trembling again.

'Try it,' she said gently. There was a very odd sound to her voice. 'See if it opens.'

'Yes, yes,' he said, breathlessly. 'Now!'

His fingers shook so much they almost let go when he started to pull the rim of the dial outwards. For a moment nothing happened, then, slowly, as if resisting his shaking hands, it began to open.

Her eyes shone queerly bright in the backglare of the light, and she began to smile. Then suddenly her smile became fixed, and she looked aside at his head.

'No!' she said suddenly. She reached out and shoved his face sideways out of range of the safe opening.

Almost at the same instant a savage crack sounded in the steel box of the safe; there was a small spit of flame in the dark mouth and something fell from the wall on the far side of the room and clattered to the floor. In the silence afterwards a small wisp of smoke came out of the safe into the torchlight.

'My God!' he whispered into his hands. Then he lifted his face and looked at her. 'You knew!'

She nodded. 'Yes. I guessed, but I was quite sure, in fact.'

He looked at the safemouth, then back to her.

'Why did you — shove me away?'

'Suddenly I didn't want it to happen.' She turned the torch into the safe.

The pistol inside was held in a vice bolted to a stout wood frame which fitted across the inside of the safe. A wire ran through little iron eye screws from the trigger, back to a pivotal eye, then forward to the safe door where it had been hooked to a bolt. The wire was slack so that when the door was closed it allowed only a crack for the setter's fingers to hook the wire to the door.

'Garner did that?'

'I guessed he'd done something,' she said. 'And this rather disproves the idea that he did know when he would die. You see, he was in no danger of being shot. He just opened the safe a little, unhooked the wire with his finger, and opened the safe wide.

'Anybody else opening it would have had his head blown off.'

He looked inside the safe.

'Whatever's there is behind the cannon,' she said. 'Can you get it out? There must be a safety catch on it. Set that first.'

He looked inside very carefully, found the catch and set it for Safe.

'The wood frame's wedged in,' he said. 'Is there anything in the bag?'

'Have a look. What sort of thing do you want?'

'Pliers would do.'

'Yes. There's a pair.'

Rayner searched in the bag and found

the tool. He began to pull out the wooden wedges which held the frame firm against the safe walls.

'How the hell did he rig this up in somebody else's safe?' he said.

'I think he rented this part of the house,' she said. 'But that's only a guess.'

She watched as he drew the murder engine carefully out of the safe. He put it on the chesterfield seat, and when he turned back the light came off him as she pointed it into the safe.

Inside was a washleather bag and a few papers. Nothing else. She took out the bag.

'Stones,' she said, and went to a small table. She emptied them out on to the polished top. 'Diamonds. So that's where the profits went.'

'Hell! what's that lot worth?'

'Enough,' she said. 'Enough for you and me. The sum of a lifetime devoted to extraction.'

He went back to the safe, using his own torch and looked at the papers.

'He rented this side of the house for a year,' he said. 'Just the rooms on this corridor. So that explains it.' He looked back at her. 'Have you any idea what they're worth? Roughly. Just roughly.'

She shrugged, staring down at them sparkling in the beam of the torch lying on the table.

'Looks like half a million,' she said. 'But don't take that too seriously. I'm no expert. But from what I do know, big sparklers like these must be way up the scale.'

'He couldn't have fiddled that much,' he said. He looked back at the empty safe then crammed the papers into his coat pocket. 'Not even over a lifetime. They must be stolen.'

'They were in the safe,' she said. 'Everything he left you pointed to that safe.'

'And the gun pointed at me,' he said. 'I don't know why you did that. You could have gone and left me here. Nobody would have known you were with me.'

'I don't know why I did it,' she said. 'In moments of tension there are revelations. It surprised me as well as you.' She began to put the stones back in the bag. 'No point in staying. Close up and go.'

'What about the gun carriage?' he said. 'Best to put it back in, and wedge it again. Hook it up and leave it.'

'But anyone could tell it's been fired,' she said, turning. 'It knocked something off the wall somewhere. Better look for that.' She took up the torch and searched the floor on the window side of the room.

She found pieces of an earthenware plate which had hung to the panelling by a wire hook. It was in many pieces. She looked at the panelling. The bullet had gone through leaving a narrow hole and a vertical split in the old wood.

'We can't cover that up. Just stuff the gun back in the safe, lock it and slide the panel over. It'll look as if Garner accidentally fired the gun while setting the trap.'

He did as she said.

They went back through the house to the main door, putting everything back as they had found it, but resetting the burglar alarm by means of the fanlight.

Throughout he let her supervise the retreat. They went back over the wall, took the rope with them and returned to the car. The night was quiet. He did nothing to break that quiet. They put the bag on the back floor.

'The tension makes one jumpy,' she said, backing along the track.

'Yes,' he said.

She turned on some night music interspersed by German jocular. That announcer was the only one who spoke during the return journey to the flats.

She drove the car into the garage and got out. He stayed in, sitting quite still.

'Come in,' she said.

'No. You've got what you wanted. I'm satisfied.'

She paused a moment.

'So the nerves have gone at last, have they? The deep black night of numbing fear grins over your muddled head. You did it. It's over. Come in. Take a drink. Or are you feeling that bullet smashing through your frontal lobes?'

He sat there. She reached in suddenly, grabbed his collar and heaved him sideways along the seat. His face hit the wheel as he went down.

'Come on,' she said, and stood back.

He just lay there. She said one short, contemptuous word, then went away to the flat.

* * *

When he walked into the flat it was twenty to two. She said nothing. Just got up from reading a magazine, went and got him a drink.

'You'll feel better,' she said.

He swallowed the drink and stared at her.

'Why did you save me?' he said.

'It just happened like that,' she said.

'No, you knew what was in there. You could have told me.'

'I wasn't going to. I was going to let it happen, but just then — well, it didn't.'

'He must have stolen those stones,' he said. 'He just couldn't have bought them!'

'Does it matter? He can't say anything. Who can?'

'He must have been a damn sight more than a crooked manager,' he said. 'Something we didn't know about, but his wife did.'

'They parted years ago. You keep forgetting that. She's just hoping there's something because she was disappointed. Besides, is this prize really a legacy? The legacy was a puzzle. That was all.'

He sat down and looked at nothing, eyes wide and vacant. Then he focussed.

'And how will they be sold?' he said, suddenly. 'Do you know anybody? A fence?'

'You didn't begin dabbling in crime for quick returns. You don't need money. I certainly don't. We should leave them for as long as seems prudent, or even longer. Then if nothing is ever heard of them, we could sell them as heirlooms, gifts, anything.'

She sat down beside him on the sofa.

'Suppose they *were* his,' she said. 'We didn't know enough about him, his fiddles, or his family or really anything but his life round here. One thing I can't imagine is Garner as a cat burglar.' She laughed.

He turned abruptly, grabbed her round the shoulders and put his other hand down the front of her shirt blouse and ripped it open.

She smiled, but, kissing her neck, he couldn't see.

★ ★ ★

The morning was fine, the air fresh, sweet and heady. He felt different. The fear of disaster had gone entirely from his mind as he went down to his father's study an hour before Mrs Colman was due to arrive. He took the envelopes from the bottom drawer and carried them to the kitchen, where the boiler was quietly burning. He opened the front and pushed in the bus timetables. After some hesitation, he put in the dollar bills, then used the tongs to get some of them out again, just to see if they were genuine.

The photographs were last, when the tables, bills and socks were burning. He opened the firedoor again, then hesitated.

He stayed a moment until the heat got unpleasant on his face, then closed the door and straightened up.

What was the point of destroying the photographs, when there were, perhaps hundreds of copies for sale, thousands had been published, and the negatives would still be alive and well in the Paris studio? And without the paraphernalia of tables, socks and the rest of it, what good were they?

He took them back into the study. Mrs Colman came as he left the room.

'There's smoke coming out of the chimney,' she said, sniffing.

'I just burnt some old papers,' he said.

'I'll get your breakfast.'

He ate a good breakfast. He felt good until, just before he should have left for the office, Mrs Garner called once more.

'Mrs Garner! What is it this time? Really, I'm getting rather tired — '

She smiled at him. It was the first time he had seen her smile. She took a case from her big bag and gave it to him.

'It's the razors,' she said.

'Oh — thank you,' he said.

'Only you weren't here last night,' she said. 'I called. Did you know your door was unlocked? The catch wasn't on. I did that.'

A cold chill came into him and began to spread.

'I was away yesterday,' he said, uneasily. 'What time did you call?'

'It was about seven, I think.'

'Oh yes. I didn't get back till late. Wasn't the housekeeper in?' he asked, watching her intently.

'Nobody at all,' she said. 'I stood in the hall and called, because as the door wasn't fixed I naturally thought somebody must be about.' She smiled again.

His heart beat fast. He could see her, finding the door open and nobody answering her calls, creeping in and through the rooms, snooping, seeing what she could find.

He was sure she knew he hadn't been in, that the door had been locked but she had got it open with a key that fitted.

How she had got that he didn't know, but it was his father's house and he didn't even know how many keys there were.

'Well, I must go,' Mrs Garner said. 'Mrs Partridge is waiting for me.'

'Mrs Partridge?' he said, sharply.

'Yes. You know. We're great friends. She drives me about because I don't myself.' She smiled. 'Good-bye.'

He watched her go down the drive and turn right to a car waiting not far along the road, then he went back into the study. He opened the desk drawer and wished he hadn't disturbed the contents earlier. Of course he had not looked to see if anyone had had them out and looked through them. There had been no reason then. Now it was too late.

Partridge's wife. Partridge. Garner, Janet and himself. All from the office. Partridge calling. Mrs Garner's repeated calling pushed from behind by an unknown woman friend. What friend? Mrs Partridge.

What did they know?

He closed the door very firmly, then used the phone to ring Janet.

'Mrs Garner called again and gave me the case of razors. The woman with her is Mrs Partridge. What's going on?'

'It's getting obvious what's going on. They think we have something and they're trying to find out what it is. But how did Partridge get to know anything just recently?'

'There could have been a message hidden in the little golf bag. He showed it to me deliberately and he gave it to you, perhaps as a joke against us. Garner may have planted a giveaway in it.'

'That could be. What else was left?'

'That bloody chair! Perhaps something's in that!'

'That's easily checked when Mann's out.'

'But what is it Garner was trying to do?'

'He was mad. You keep forgetting that. He was a real split. He kept the black side for when he was alone. He didn't often show anything in the office. He was just an eccentric, but it fitted the business. Outside it he was very different. You didn't really know that side of him.

I did. What's in the razors? Oh! I didn't give you the key. I'll call on my way.'

She rang off.

Mrs Colman opened the door and looked in.

'You'll be late. Can I do in here?'

'Not yet. Miss Hayworth is bringing some letters.'

Mrs Colman nodded and went out. 'Bit early in the day, for me, anyways,' she told the hall clock as she dusted it. When Janet arrived, the woman showed her into the study.

Rayner closed the door firmly and led Janet over to the windows.

'She got in here last night and nosed around, the Garner woman,' he said.

'She wouldn't have known where to look to find anything,' Janet said. 'Here's the key. Be careful when you open it.'

He was very careful putting the key into the small lock. It would not turn. He tried again, then took the key out and looked at it. He tried a third time and still the key would not turn.

'Leave it!' he said angrily. 'You go ahead.'

She nodded and left. He put the case in the bottom drawer, went out, got his car and drove to the office. As he locked his car in the park behind the building, Freda Jarvis spoke from just beside him.

'I'm not hounding you,' she said. 'But something has cropped up.'

He looked at her with anxiety showing in his face. She was pleased to see it.

'It's quite crazy, perhaps,' she went on, 'but I had a phone call this morning from a man who said that you murdered this man Garner for some money which was in the office that night, but which the police never found out about. I thought you should know.'

She went to go.

'A man?' he said.

She looked back a moment. 'Yes. Did you think it might be a woman?' She laughed and went to her car.

He watched her without really seeing anything real. The world had taken on a dreamlike quality where nothing was solid, nothing capable of hurting, just not capable of being. He shook his head as if some kind of infection was causing the mental haze, but it persisted.

In his office he went through his work mechanically, until suddenly the message from Freda took on a frightening urgency. He went into Janet's office, as usual, taking a handful of papers with him.

She looked up at him as he closed the door behind him and looked towards Mann's door. That, too, was shut.

'What's the matter?' she said. 'You look ill.'

He told her what Freda had said.

'An anonymous call,' she said, and shrugged. 'Worrying, but not disaster. The fact that it's true needn't mean the call isn't a black joke. You never told me how much was in the chair.'

'Eleven thousand.' He seemed glad to be rid of the secret at last.

She looked at him coolly, eyes keen behind her almond shaped glasses.

'Are you trying to sell yourself to me?' she said. 'Or have you some idea I am in it with you?'

'No. I — ' He stared. 'Well, we are

in it now, aren't we?'

'You would have difficulty in proving anything against me, wouldn't you?' she said, and began to make a phone call. 'Just think that over at your leisure — if you have much,' she ended, covering the mouthpiece with her hand. 'Hallo? Sanderson-Wickes? Yes . . . '

He went back to his office, trying to think of what she had said, but he could only remember one bit then, not another, doubted the first, and then began to doubt his own head. He was getting in a mess trying to think. Her cold attitude had plunged him deep in despair. He had thought she would help him against Freda and the anonymous caller, but she didn't want to know.

He was beginning to float in a black slough, just hoping that somewhere ahead would be a landing stage.

He tried, once, to make out why he had been so confident only a few days ago, but now apparently was surrounded by people meaning harm.

He got up from his desk suddenly and walked out of the office and the building.

He hardly noticed driving back to the house. Mrs Colman had gone home to lunch. The house was deserted. He went to the gardening shed and found an old chisel of his father's. He went back into the study and broke open the razor case.

They were all there, the seven razors but not in their marked places. They were jumbled together at one end of the case to make way for a small tape recorder.

He stared at the little machine as if it might be a time bomb. Several times he put out his finger to the 'Play' button and then drew it back. He knew what it would be: Garner talking from a time just before that open grave when he first felt Janet was watching him.

And the reading of the will, when he had felt her watching him from under that little veil, sideglances, seeing how he reacted to the words — The words — What words? The final words. The last words.

' — which will help him to decide whether he shall continue with a life of criminal ingratitude or cut his throat.'

Cut his throat. The final words. Of course. The razors. All there in the box. One for the right day — Monday. He sorted through the razors until he found the one with Monday carved into the white bone handle. He picked it up and opened the blade. It was gleaming as new. He read the engraved name 'Kropp' as if it were some friendly message.

He threw the razor back into the box and stood up with a jerk.

Suicide? What on earth was the point of that? How in hell had he sunk so far from his senses to fondle such an idea?

He heard the doorbell ring. It sounded several times. He went out quickly to keep it quiet. Janet was there. She just walked in. He closed the door. She walked on through the open doorway of the study. A moment's hesitation, then he followed.

'Shut the door,' she said.

He shut it. She looked at the open box, the razors and the tape machine.

'What's the matter with you? Walking out like that! You attract attention all the time! Can't you get it into your head?'

'It was that phone call Freda said — '

'Well? Who do you think it was? Garner, loud-hailing across the Styx? Think! It's someone who has it in for you because he thinks you have something he should have had.'

He started to pace. 'Partridge. He does imitations. Partridge rang her up. He knew about Freda. Everybody knows about it. Somebody spread it round — '

'Shut up.' She sat down at the desk looking at the razor case. 'I suppose you think this tape is Garner telling of something happening that ended with his death?' She sat back. 'It can't be that, now, can it? Cut through the panic and start thinking sensibly.'

'Why did you come after me?' he said, watching her, almost gratefully.

'It's my job to keep you quiet,' she said. 'Well, let's see what the man says.' She pushed down the 'Play' button.

The thin small voice was Garner's. It began a tirade of such fury, such hate, such blinding, boiling rage, such foul language, worse invention and appalling imagery that Rayner stood with his mouth half open, shattered by shock and confused emotions.

The bawling ended abruptly with 'Goodbye, you filthy — !' as if the ranter had choked himself with hate.

Rayner stayed stunned by the realisation that nowhere had the dead man mentioned a threat of murder. The spasm had been a burst of hatred against himself and Janet.

'Why?' Rayner said blankly.

Janet shrugged. 'I keep telling you, his drive belts had come off. That he could have kept on the job without it being noticed shows control, or maybe just mad cunning. I'm not a psychiatrist. I couldn't tell the difference. But he did all these things and if you think that the puzzle he left was a sane man's idea of confusing an issue, then we divide once more. Come on back to the office. Don't attract attention by behaving like a quivering leaf.'

She got up. She looked at him for a second, then went.

When she had gone he played the

tape again, as if a replay released him from some awful fear. The tone of the voice was demented. It began to puzzle him. Why had the man been so viciously hating and then left something which must have been precious to his own dreams?

The tape was running as he tried to sort out his thoughts on the paradox. As he reached out to switch it off, the voice began again, speaking in a flat, weary tone.

'My dear Rayner,' it said, 'by the time you hear this I shall be dead and you will be my murderer. I have arranged things so that this must be so.

'I have known for some time that there is something wrong with me; a final confirmation was given to me by my specialist, and my time is measurable in months, numbering, at most eighteen. It is a growth in the brain, dear fellow, which at present rate will prove terminal in the time stated. Given that, a little fun is permissible for me, I think. You may call it a macabre sort of game, planning for you to kill me, but I have nothing to lose, and the unexpectedness of a sudden death seems preferable, to me now, to looking at a set date, like the buffers at the end of a railway line.

'So I left certain signs under your nose that I was embezzling company funds, and usually checked — for myself — every Thursday evening alone, and so on. Of course you took that in, and how you finally carried it out, I don't know, of course, but I knew you would. I long decided that you, basically, were the material of ruthless management, of criminal potential, without conscience or compassion, but also, without courage. You are and always will be, a bloody coward, Rayner. I know all these things because you are unbalanced, frustrated, oppressed by a superior father to a hatred of father figures, and this, and almost everything else that passes within you, shows on your limpid face when you don't take care. And you don't take anything like enough care.

'I have had great fun composing a puzzle for you which will lead you to a fortune, if you can solve it that far, but

I am sure that my dearest Janet will help you in overcoming the cowardice which may otherwise stop you getting through. Indeed, I have asked her to do so.

'I think, as you hear this, you should have got the prize, which isn't mine, I should explain, but the treasure of Lord Malling, hidden from the taxman and taking the shape of undeclared profits improperly translated into stone.

'As you hear me now, then you missed the shot, which I also had fun in arranging. Fun? Macabre? Why so, Rayner? With the time at my disposal and funds to assist my whims, I found my predicament has lifted me out of the normal world of confines and rails, and allowed me to enjoy the eccentric world between convention and finality.

'And of course, dear boy, the greatest joke comes last, but by the time you appreciate it you'll be as dead as I am.'

'Goodbye, Rayner. Many thanks.'

Rayner sat watching the small machine as if it were alive. It ran on, hissing softly. Then he jumped up.

'Crazy! He was crazy as a coot! How

the hell could he have worked it all out like that and be sure — ?'

And as if the machine still spoke he seemed to hear someone say, 'Because he knew you. He says he knew you. He made a point of saying what you were, how weak you were, where you could give way and why.'

Rayner turned and snapped off the tape switch.

There was, of course, a simple way out. Go. Get away. He had eleven thousand pounds from the chair seat, enough to get right away and start again . . . But if he went, people would begin to think, and to talk, and then to point, and then the police would move, and gradually, on the domino principle, police force after police force would be alerted and soon there would be nowhere to run.

Because Freda would say what the man had told her on the phone, and Partridge would speak up the message Garner had left him to give, and the widow might have heard the tape — or even have a copy —

But that was the coward talking. Of

course he could go, change name, appearance, life —

And all of it would show on his face. Whatever name, whatever life, whatever pretence, James Elroy Rayner would shine through clearly, written on his face as Garner had seen it, as Janet had seen it —

He sat down and stared at the small machine and the razors, and his old, familiar depression began to creep up inside him and convince him that he must lose.

The sound of the door bell ripped through his head like a shot. He just sat, staring at the razors. Then he put the machine back in the case and shut it.

The doorbell rang again. He put the case in the lower drawer of the desk and sat back in the chair, trying to think.

The doorbell rang a third time. He reached down, opened the drawer, flipped the case lid open and took out one of the razors.

He heard the front door open. He must have knocked the loose catch again, the one that had let Mrs Garner in. He stood up with the razor in his hand.

'Rayner! Rayner? Are you in?'

'Partridge!' said Rayner, staring at nothing.

* * *

'Forasmuch as it hath pleased Almighty God of his great mercy, to take unto himself the soul of the dear brother here departed — '

She looked down at the oblong hole in the ground, and the feet of the mourners around it. The short black veil she wore softened the harshness of a scene which seemed so out of place on such a lovely day.

Not that she was sad. Not sad, as she had been when standing by Garner's grave. She had really been a mourner then.

Of course, they would catch him, but why he had run she could not think. What good could it do him? He was bound to be caught — unless he jumped off a cliff. He might do that.

Of course, there were humourous bits

about it, especially when the police searched the study and found the old gentleman's selection of pornographic pictures, but that's what old gentlemen sometimes collected.

' . . . ashes to ashes, dust to dust . . . '

Of course, there had been the idea in his mind that Partridge was a threat, specially when he realised the widow's companion was Mrs Partridge, but even so — Why on earth had he killed Partridge when, by ordinary logic, he should have killed himself?

Perhaps she and her lover had had the wrong slant on cowards somewhere in their reckoning.

THE END

We do hope that you have enjoyed reading this large print book.

Did you know that all of our titles are available for purchase?

We publish a wide range of high quality large print books including:
Romances, Mysteries, Classics, General Fiction, Non Fiction and Westerns.

Special interest titles available in large print are:
The Little Oxford Dictionary Music Book, Song Book Hymn Book, Service Book

Also available from us courtesy of Oxford University Press:
Young Readers' Dictionary (large print edition) Young Readers' Thesaurus (large print edition)

For further information or a free brochure, please contact us at:
Ulverscroft Large Print Books Ltd., The Green, Bradgate Road, Anstey, Leicester, LE7 7FU, England. Tel: (00 44) 0116 236 4325
Fax: (00 44) 0116 234 0205

Other titles in the
Linford Mystery Library:

SIDEWINDER

Jane Morell

Lisette, a British agent sent to the Lebanon to extricate an American hostage, disappears without trace, leaving behind a husband and a young son, Robert. Ten years later, Robert tracks down her betrayer, intent on revenge. Winton, the man responsible, has made a new life for himself in Wales. However, Robert doesn't count on meeting Winton's daughter, Sara. How can he murder the father of the girl he has come to love? But is Sara the innocent creature she appears to be?